Nightfall Gardens

ALLEN HOUSTON

COVER ILLUSTRATION: ANTHONY ROBERTS

Nightfall Gardens: Book One
ISBN -10: 0615804454
ISBN-13: 978-0615804454

For Imogen always and my godson Silas

ALLEN HOUSTON

CONTENTS

Nightfall Gardens

1

The Amazing Blackwoods

Only later, when she was locked away at Nightfall Gardens, would Lily realize that the moment she saw the man with the wolf's-head cloak was the beginning of the end of her old life.

Tonight, though, her biggest concern was finishing the rest of the performance.

"Line!" Celeus Talbot demanded. The old actor swayed drunkenly onto the stage of the Golden Bough Theater. In his time, Talbot had been the greatest actor of his generation, playing Dr. Faustus and Hamlet before kings and queens. A love of the bottle ruined him and now he spent his days deep in rotgut whiskey and his nights calling out for lines he no longer bothered memorizing.

"It'll bring great prestige to have him on the bill," her father, Thomas, told the family when he introduced the besotted actor to them. Lily looked at her mother, Moira, and brother, Silas, who raised one eyebrow skeptically. "This will put us on the map at last."

That was her father, always the optimist. They could play the dingiest gin halls or grimiest vaudeville stages and he believed that they were one step from "making it." The Amazing Blackwood Family tops the bill at long last.

"Are thee prepardest to spend life under the sea?" Moira pitched the line from offstage. Lily saw her mother out of the corner of her eye holding the script her father had written.

Celeus Talbot staggered toward the young girl, who was tied to a wooden beam with a papier-mâché chain. For a second, he nearly stumbled into the hole in the center of the stage.

"Isn't she grand," her father exclaimed when the family first saw the dilapidated theater with its creaking stage, worn velvet seats and oil-encrusted walls where the lamp racks left stains on the wallpaper. The worst part was the hole in the stage floor. "Just make sure and step around it," he warned. "Think of it as a test of your acting ability." The Golden Bough might have been "grand" 100 years ago, but now it was just another bottom-of-the-barrel fire hazard for third-rate acting troupes.

"Are thee preparedest to eat my fleas," Celeus slurred.

Someone in the audience guffawed. A tomato flew out of the darkness and splattered against the backdrop.

"Line!" Celeus barked. He was close enough that Lily smelled his rancid breath. The old actor's eyes were cracked hard-boiled eggs behind the gray makeup supposed to make him look like a sea monster, but which made him look like a dejected chimney sweep.

"Then down to the ocean we go," Moira called behind the curtain.

"Down we must go!" Celeus thundered. He raised his index finger in sharp exclamation and immediately thrust it over his mouth to keep from vomiting.

"Hee hee, the salty dog's had one too many," a gruff voice heckled from the audience.

"Only way he can make it through this rubbish, innit?" someone called back.

Another tomato whizzed out of the dark. This one barely missed Celeus who was listing like a pummeled prizefighter about to go down for the count.

Lily looked into the audience and saw the usual bowler hats, winking cigars, and irate wives trying to stuff some culture down their husbands' throats. Most of the seats were empty. A homeless man was asleep in the front row. He was spread out across several seats, slack-jawed, one sock on, one off. His suit jacket was balled under his head for a pillow. In the back of the theater, a card game was taking place.

The man in the second row stood out over the

others as though lit by his own incandescence. A mane of white hair fell to his shoulders. His face was gaunt. Ice blue eyes stared out of hollowed sockets. A puckered scar ran from the side of his mouth to his ear. Most amazing of all was the wolf's-hide cloak he wore. The head, which doubled as a hood, was thrown casually over his shoulder. It must have been a magnificent beast when it was alive. Inch-long fangs stuck out of the gaping maw of its mouth. The man caught Lily staring and didn't turn away.

His eyes made her uncomfortable. She glanced toward the curtain where her brother Silas was jotting down lines with a quill and foolscap paper.

'Please, not this time,' she thought. Her brother had been so consumed with his writing yesterday that he missed his cue. Lily stalled the restless crowd by dancing a jig while dodging tomatoes and flying ale steins.

Silas must have sensed how poorly the performance was going. He looked up at that moment, set his papers aside and strode on to the stage.

"Here comes Little Lord Fauntleroy," one of the audience hooted. Laughter echoed off the cavernous walls of the Golden Bough.

Lily had to admit her little brother *did* look unusual. He was all skin and bones with a rat's nest of black hair that no amount of tonic could tame. He towered inches above the other children his age. His eyes were his oddest characteristic. One was blue and one was brown. That never failed to draw comment from those meeting him for the first time. *"Well, I've never seen anything like that before." "Are you sure he's all right?"*

"Unhand her, beast of the deep! Beautiful Andromeda will go nowhere with you," Silas commanded Celeus who was attempting to take the papier-mâché chains off of her. The white robes her brother wore were two sizes too large.

"How about going somewhere with me, love?" a player in the card game called to Lily. She hoped no one could see her blush in the darkened theater.

"Line!" Celeus thundered. He finally managed to work the fake chains free and grabbed Lily by the arm.

"Brave Perseus, prepare to meet thy doom," Moira said from off-stage.

"What?" Celeus said. He cupped his ear so he could hear better.

"Brave Perseus, prepare to meet thy doom," she repeated.

"Perseus, ready for doom," he mumbled.

Fake swords were drawn. Silas and Celeus clashed and clanged the props together. At one point, the old actor took a wild swing at Silas. The young boy ducked, and Celeus stumbled behind the curtain long enough to down half a pint of whiskey before roaring back on the stage.

The alcohol reinvigorated the old actor and he began improvising lines.

"Let's see you dodge this," Celeus said. He

lunged at the young boy, who stepped out of the way. The thespian was angry now. "I'll spill your blood and steal your rotting sister," he hissed.

The audience came alive for the first time. Blood fever overtook them. "Take his head off, you old git!" A man in a bowler stood and shouted. "Maim him, boy!" a woman in a black dress called. The people playing cards began to place bets on who would win the fight.

With a final bellow, Celeus charged Silas, who feinted and smacked the actor on the backside as he hurtled off the stage into the orchestra pit. Groans issued from the injured man.

The audience went wild, stamping their feet in approval until mortar shook from the walls of the Golden Bough. Silas and Lily exchanged a look. It wasn't supposed to go like this, not at all. There was still another act to the play. Celeus's groans grew louder from the pit.

"Somebody help me out of here," the great thespian whimpered. "I think I broke my leg."

"Now!" Moira said. Silas and Lily exchanged nervous glances, took each other's hands and bowed to the audience. Laughter and thunderous applause continued as the moth-eaten curtain whisked across the stage.

Their mother was waiting for them as they exited into the wings. Behind the curtain, they heard the audience shuffling toward the doors.

"Always exit while you're on top," their mother said, giving them a gentle smile.

"I suppose I should make sure Mr. Talbot can climb out of the orchestra pit," Silas groused.

His mother looked at him as if it wasn't an option. "He's an old man who has nothing left but his pride," she said. "Help him out and tell him we're adding 10 percent to his pay tonight."

Silas opened his mouth as if to say something and then bit down on his lip. He slipped around the curtain, leaving the two of them alone.

"Let me help you with your makeup," Moira said. The dressing room where the actors changed was packed with costumes from various performances from over the decades, a make-up counter and a bubbled mirror so old that it glowed.

"Horrible, absolutely awful," Lily said. She dropped into a chair in front of the mirror and crossed her arms.

"Oh, it wasn't that bad," Moira said as she began removing Lily's makeup.

"No, I suppose Mr. Talbot made it to the second act before he fell off the stage," Lily fumed. "Father promised when we moved to New Amsterdam we wouldn't have to play places like *this*."

"Places like what?" Moira said. Color flushed her cheeks and Lily could tell her mother was angry.

"Honestly, mother," Lily swept her hands around the room. "Places where mold doesn't grow on the walls, where you might fall through a hole in the stage or be pelted by a tomato or play to an empty theater. He promised this town would be different."

"New Amsterdam is a large city. It takes a while to get established. Things will change, you'll see." Moira scrubbed roughly at the make up on her daughter's face.

"You say that every time, and every time before we can make a name for ourselves we move to the next city. I don't understand why we can't settle down somewhere. Do you know how hard it is for Silas and me to make friends?"

Canaan, Harwich, Barrington, Freetown, Ipswich, Sudbury and Weymouth. The list of cities where they lived was long and the number of backwood provinces that they toured was longer. Every two years, for all of Lily's 13 years, the Blackwood family had up rooted and moved on to the next town. They never stayed long enough to make friends or feel that any place was home.

Moira's eyes softened and she stroked her daughter's face. Lily was tall for her age, with white-blond hair that curled past her shoulders. Her skin was the color of cream, except for her red lips and pale blue eyes. Perfect seashell ears stuck out of the foam of her hair.

"I know how hard this must be for —" Moira started.

"You don't know any such thing," Lily shouted. "Otherwise you wouldn't put us through it." She pushed her mother's hand away and furiously began brushing her own hair.

"If you had any idea what your father has

sacrificed for your sake, you wouldn't say such things," her mother said.

"Him? He's as much a foolish dreamer as my brother," Lily said. "He can't act, write or balance the books, yet we're the Amazing Blackwoods." She laughed at the irony of that.

"Don't," Moira said and the fire was back in her eyes. "Don't say that about him."

"Why? I'm not saying anything you don't already know," Lily said. She walked to the door.

"Where do you think you're going?" her mother demanded.

"*Some* of us have fans to greet," Lily said stomping out of the room.

No matter how poorly the performance went, a trickle of fans would wait behind the back of the theater for the autograph of the beautiful girl with white hair. Tonight was no different. A smattering of people stood on the cobblestone street, huddled in hats and scarves and blowing on their hands to keep warm. A thin yellow moon floated large above the alley.

"Outstanding performance, miss. Outstanding!" a man so fat that his cravat couldn't be tied said.

"Brilliant, you brought me to tears," a woman with no chin in a cinched black coat said and then whispered. "I always fancied myself an actress."

Lily signed autographs and told them to come back next week, when the Amazing Blackwoods would perform the works of Euripides. She waited until everyone left and was about to go back inside when a rough voice came from a darkened doorway across the street.

"One more autograph," the man with the wolf cloak said, stepping into the threadbare light of the moon. The wolf's head had been pulled over him like a hat and its eyes burned gold. Only the bottom half of his face and the scar near his mouth were visible. His lips turned up into a harsh smile.

"I — I have to go," Lily said. She didn't know why, but her heart was hammering in her chest and for some reason she felt very frightened. She grabbed the door to open it, but the man in the cloak slammed it shut. Lily shrank against the wall.

"Is that any way to treat someone who's come such a long way to see you?" he asked.

"Who are you?" Lily replied, trying to keep the fear out of her voice.

He released the door and stepped away from her. He smiled again and his teeth curved into fangs in the moonlight.

"Who am I? Why, I'm your uncle. I'm your dear father's brother, Jonquil."

2
Coming of Final Night

"Where's the other half of my rent? I'm not in the habit of running a charity," Gideon Wassum grumbled. He slapped a pair of sheepskin-lined leather gloves down on the desk where Thomas Blackwood was counting that night's receipts.

Wassum, the portly owner of the Golden Bough, wore a silk top hat and his puffy cheeks rolled like jelly over his shirt collar. He drew a wooden box out of his coat and expertly removed a pinch of snuff and snorted it, his eyes glazing over and nostrils flaring. "I've had freeloaders before and they all end up the same way — out in the cold!"

"I assure you, Mr. Wassum, you'll receive your rent," Thomas said. "We just need time to get established here."

"You need more than time if tonight's performance was any indication," Wassum said.

11

He peeked over Thomas's shoulder at the accounts ledger. "Why, you didn't even break even!"

"Mr. Wassum —."

"One more week," the owner said holding up a beefy finger. "And then say goodbye to the Golden Bough Theater."

The owner waddled out of the room, slamming the door behind him. Thomas put his head in his hands and rubbed his tired eyes.

Silas watched through a grate in the wall. When he was certain they were finished, he slowly closed the vent and padded away so his father wouldn't hear.

He had discovered the tunnels that ran from the theater to the sewer the week before while moving props in the storeroom. As he stacked boxes of wigs, fake mustaches, and costume jewelry he uncovered a dusty trap door. Taking a candle, Silas descended a wooden ladder into the underbelly of the city. Tunnels led in every direction. Candlelight reflected off stone walls before it was sucked away by darkness. A breeze stirred somewhere ahead. Rotting barrels smelling of rum were lined up along the wall. *'Must have been used by bootleggers,'* he thought.

He spent the rest of the afternoon exploring the tunnels, following them until they came out into the sewer, where he saw a white rat with volcanic red eyes that was the size of a small dog and decided to go no further. Some of the passages were eerily illuminated by light that seeped from vents along the wall. The youngest Blackwood realized he could see and hear everything going on inside if he was close enough to those grates, even those things he didn't want to.

'What are we going to do?' Silas thought. Things were even worse than expected. If they didn't pay rent the next week, they were going to be kicked out and then it would be on to the next town. *'I'll tell Lily,'* he thought. His sister was vain but she was also his only friend.

Silas felt along the slick stone of the walls as he followed his way back to the prop room. He stopped only when he heard sobbing coming from the dressing room. He peeked through the vent to discover his mother crying.

Lily thought she was, but in truth, their mother was the most beautiful Blackwood. Moira's red hair tangled dark as fire around her shoulders. Experience stamped her features where his sister's face was unmarred by anything other than egotism. The men were drab by comparison. His father was tall and too thin, with the same uncontrollable churn of black hair as his son. Round spectacles pinched his nose. *'At least he looks normal,'* Silas thought. His blue and brown eyes marked him for bullies as sure as any sign he could carry.

He watched his mother with a growing sense of helplessness and climbed back into the prop room. A paper dragon, yellow with red scales, hung the length of the ceiling and stared down at him. Backdrops, costumes, fake weapons, furniture, and an old cannon filled the rest of the room.

Silas picked up his quill, inkpot, and parchment from where he left them. It was the beginning of a play he was writing to surprise his family. Perhaps it would be the blockbuster that would finally lift them out of poverty.

He was thinking on this when he stepped from the room and into the path of his sister and a strange man wearing a wolf's-head cloak. The man was gripping her by the arm.

"Lily?" Silas asked. His sister was paler than usual. There was fear behind her soft blue eyes.

"Si — Silas. Thank goodness," she said.

"Who is this man?" he said, ignoring the glare from her companion.

"This *man* is your Uncle Jonquil," the man said. "And my business isn't with you, boy. I need to see my brother."

"Uncle? Father doesn't have any brothers," Silas said.

Jonquil grunted a laugh. "Told you that, did he? Can't say I blame him. Thought he was well good and clear of me."

Silas saw the blotch of red on his sister where the man was squeezing her arm.

"Is he hurting you?" he asked Lily.

"I'll *hurt* you if you don't get out of my way, boy," Jonquil said. "Didn't anyone teach you to respect time?"

He pushed past Silas towards Thomas's office. "Thomas, Moira, dear old Jonquil has come home at last," his uncle bellowed. He dragged Lily along like she was made of feathers.

"Let — go — of — me," Lily demanded, trying to yank her arm away.

"Feisty. Your grandmother will like that," Jonquil said. He reached the office door and kicked it, splintering the jamb as he entered to the shocked expression on their father's face. "Never thought you'd see me again, did you?" Jonquil said. His smile was as sharp as a fresh razor.

"Jonquil!" Thomas grabbed for a derringer on his cluttered desk. He pointed the pearl handled pistol at the giant.

"Put that pea shooter away before you irritate me. I came to talk," Jonquil said. He released Lily, who stepped away, rubbing her bruised arm. Silas watched from the doorway.

"You found us," Thomas said. He lowered the gun but kept it cocked.

"A merry chase you led as well. As soon as I'd get wind, you were on to the next town."

"But why? You gave your word you wouldn't follow us," Thomas said.

"That's a promise I'd just as soon have kept," Jonquil said. The light reflected off the glass wolf eyes on his cloak. "Dark times are on us though. There was no choice."

Silas and Lily exchanged a look across the room. *'He's mad,'* Silas thought.

At that moment, Moira burst into the room. Her eyes were swollen from crying but otherwise she was more beautiful than ever. "Thomas, what's making that racket?" She froze when she saw Jonquil on the other side of the room.

The giant pushed the wolf hood back from his head. His white hair glowed. The ragged scar on his cheek pulsated with life.

"Jonquil, you've —," Moira stumbled for words.

"Gotten old, I know," he said. "The minutes move quickly in the dusk."

'What does that mean?' Silas thought. Why had their father never told him about his brother? Thomas and Moira were orphans at a workhouse for the poor. They escaped and were taken in by kindly Professor Prendergast and his Amazing Traveling Theater Spectacle. That was where they learned how to act and perform. How many times had Silas and Lily been told that story? Was that a lie as well?

"Children, go to your rooms and wait," Thomas said. He stood and towered over his brother, though Jonquil was twice as wide. "I'll explain later."

He shooed Lily and Silas toward the door. Moira put her hands on their shoulders. "I'm sure this seems confusing, but you must trust us. There is much we haven't told you — for your own safety," she said.

"Wait," Jonquil commanded. Moira and the children stopped in their treks. "There's no time for niceties. This concerns the girl. She needs to hear this."

"Me?" Lily said shocked.

'How could any of this possibly involve her?' Silas thought. *'Until ten minutes ago we didn't even know we had an uncle.'*

"Silas, Lily, go to your room. I'll —," Thomas began.

"Deiva is dying," Jonquil said. His words cut through the room. Thomas collapsed into his chair. Moira loosened her grip on the children.

"It can't be," Thomas said. His voice was a croak.

"Oh, I'm afraid so," Jonquil said. "The reaper comes for us all in the end."

"Who's Deiva?" Lily asked their mother.

"It's — it's your grandmother," their mother said.

"We have a grandmother?" Lily said. This was growing more puzzling by the moment.

"Aye. Her blood courses through your veins," their uncle said. "And that's what brings me here."

"What happened?" Thomas asked quietly. His face crumpled and black circles hid his eyes.

"Gilirot," Jonquil said. "It's ate half her face away. She doesn't have long."

"Is she still —."

"Waiting for father to come home from the long ride?" Jonquil sneered. "Every day she sees his ghost approaching from her upstairs window and every day she tells the servants to ready the great hall for a feast. He never makes it from the mist, you know this. She's grown madder with each year

17

that passes."

Silas watched Thomas as he paced the room in great strides. He had never seen him like this. His father was normally unflappable — 'too gentle hearted' was what their mother said. His face danced with emotion. He chewed his nails.

"Why did you come here?" Thomas finally burst out.

"You know why," Jonquil said. His face grew hard as stone. "For the girl."

"No!" Moira said. She threw her arms around Lily.

"Blackwood women have always ruled Nightfall Gardens, going back before the written word," Jonquil said.

"You could take charge," Moira burst out. "It's what you've always wanted."

Jonquil sneered. "You think so little of me, eh? I've done my duty keeping the dark at bay for 13 years, but it draws closer with each sip of Deiva's faltering breath. Only a Blackwood daughter can keep the final night from coming. You know that as well as I."

"Children, go to your rooms. Now!" Thomas banged his fist so hard on his desk that his inkpot jumped. Pieces of parchment fluttered to the ground. "Your uncle and I have much to discuss."

Moira leaned down to talk to them. She looked ten years older in the glow of candlelight. "I'll explain everything later," she said. "It's a story I never wished to tell."

This time Jonquil said nothing as the children were pushed out of the room and the door closed.

"What was that all about?" Lily said in a huff. She balled her fists on her slender hips. "Do you think that horrible man's really our uncle? What's all that blather about us having a grandmother? What's Nightfall Gardens?"

"I don't know, but I have an idea how we can find out," Silas said. He led his sister to the prop room, where they climbed down into the tunnels.

Muffled voices came from the vent in their father's office. Silas opened it and bars of light checkered Lily's face. "Why didn't you tell me about this?" his sister mouthed. Silas shrugged.

The voices were clear now and they could see into the office. Their father and mother were behind the desk, and Jonquil was facing in a chair opposite.

"I take no pleasure in this," their uncle said. "But the gates will close in three more days and when they finally re-open, I'm afraid Deiva will be dead."

"We left that world behind," Moira said.

"You never leave behind the place you came from," Jonquil said. "Especially Nightfall Gardens. If the dark should escape, no one will be safe."

"An old wives' tale," Thomas said. "Meant to scare us when we were children."

"Things have changed. Our mother was powerful then, but now she grows weak. The plowmen see red-eyed things in the dusk. A three-headed calf was born to the miller in Priortage. The mist comes closer and closer to the Gardens. New rooms appear in the house, each with something horrible to behold."

"Lock the gate, throw away the key and let Nightfall Gardens crumble to the earth like it should have centuries ago," Thomas said.

"And what about the people of the mist? What happens to them?" Jonquil said. "What happens if the gate buckles and the darkness escapes?"

Heavy silence fell between the three of them. A spider scuttled over the back of Silas's neck and he almost screamed in surprise. Lily grabbed his hand and squeezed.

Moira was the first to break the quiet. "You ask for the impossible. We left Nightfall Gardens exactly because we couldn't condemn our daughter to what awaited her."

"No, instead you'd rather doom everyone else," Jonquil said scornfully. He pulled a leather bag from under his cloak. "Mother said to give you this," he tossed the sack and it landed with a thump on the desk. "Consider what I told you. I'm staying at the Bucket of Blood tonight and tomorrow I head back north. Gods help us all if Nightfall Gardens should fall because of your arrogance." With a whisk of his cloak, Jonquil turned and was gone.

Their mother put her arms around their father and kissed him on the forehead.

"What if what he says is true?" Thomas said.

"It can't be. Living in perpetual dusk does funny things to a person," Moira said. "You remember how mad they are. Why do you think Jonquil helped us escape when your mother tried to take Lily?"

"But I saw shapes in the Gardens, and the house — I swear it was alive," Thomas said. "How can you forget what happened in the tunnels? What about the attic?"

"Don't talk about that!" Moira said.

Silas and Lily exchanged another glance. They heard fear in their mother's voice.

She continued. "We left because of what that place was and what Deiva would do to our daughter. You heard your brother. The gate closes in three days and then it won't open again for another year. All we have to do is wait."

Thomas picked up the bag Jonquil had left. He opened the drawstring and poured out the contents. Gold coins, yellow as butter, spilled on to the desk. Their father held up one of the coins.

"My mother thinks to buy our daughter from us," he said examining it.

"Send it back," Moira said. "We made a vow to protect Lily from that evil woman and Nightfall Gardens."

Their father scooped the coins back in to the bag. Thomas sighed. "Let's check on the children. We'll tell them as much as we dare in the morrow."

Silas and Lily climbed back up the ladder into the prop room.

"What do you think it all means?" Lily asked, right before they separated.

Silas shook his head. "It sounds like something out of one of father's plays."

They exchanged goodnights and rushed to their rooms. Silas had barely slipped under the blanket on the straw mattress where he slept, when the door cracked and his parents stared in at him.

"I promise we'll tell you more about your uncle and grandmother in the morning. We wouldn't have lied to you without good reason," Thomas said.

The door closed and Silas was left with his thoughts. He lay there a long while before he took quill and parchment and began writing by the forlorn moon hanging over New Amsterdam. He wrote long into the night, puzzling over why his parents hadn't told them about his family. A thud came from his sister's room, followed by a door opening. Silas stopped writing and listened. Heavy footsteps creaked down the hall. What was Lily doing up this late? She slept like a rock even during the most trying times.

Silas lit a candle and got dressed. Something didn't feel right. He opened his door, the candle's flame sputtered tall on the walls. He looked both ways but saw nothing. From outside, he thought he heard a horse whinnying.

"Lily," he said, before opening her door. No one answered. He saw what was wrong as soon as he entered. The trunk holding all of her belongings was gone.

Before his tired mind could piece together what was happening, Silas heard raised voices from outside. He ran to the window and saw Jonquil dragging his sister toward a carriage. Two men wearing wolf cloaks sat on the clapboard, holding the reins of a pair of gigantic black horses.

Silas took off running for the prop room and the hidden tunnels beneath the city. He had to stop them. *They were trying to kidnap his sister.*

3

A Space In-Between

Lily was dreaming of a faceless crowd tossing roses at her feet on a great stage in Paris when a hand pressed against her mouth and she woke to Jonquil standing over her.

"Quiet, dear niece, unless you'd soon be without a brother and parents," her uncle whispered. "Don't make me do something I'd rather not."

Lily nodded in understanding. Her heart fluttered like a moth trapped in a glass, pounding against her ribs until she thought it would break free. Two hard men wearing the same style of cloak as Jonquil stood mute in the shadows.

Her uncle pulled his hand away and gestured for them to take her trunk. Silently, they lifted the chest and left the room.

'What should I do?' Lily thought. *'Why doesn't Silas wake up and hear what's happening?'*

"Get dressed," Jonquil spoke into her ear. "And no noises if you wish your family to live."

Her uncle retreated to the window, where he stared out onto the cobblestoned streets of New Amsterdam. If he had any doubt about whether Lily would try to alert her brother or parents, none of it showed on his cruel face.

A simple blue dress had been left at the foot of her bed. *'He's thought of everything,'* she thought. What would happen if she screamed loud enough to wake her father and mother? What could they do against three men? What if there were more lurking outside? Lily slipped into the dress and tried calming herself. The best thing would be to go with him. Her parents would know where they were taking her.

Jonquil led her out of the Golden Bough and to the street. Her uncle's men were sitting on the driver's seat of a mud-spattered horse-drawn carriage. Black curtains were pulled over the windows.

'In there,' he said, pushing her towards the carriage. She gave one brief glance at Silas's window, but it was empty. The inside of the carriage was lined with red velvet. Jonquil squeezed into the seat across from her. He was so big that his head almost touched the ceiling. He tapped on the roof of the carriage and a moment later it rolled away down the street.

"I would rather not have done it this way, but there's no time for pleasantries," her uncle said as the carriage jounced over the rocky street. "While your parents are wringing their hands, Nightfall Gardens is collapsing."

"Is that where we're going?" Lily asked.

"Aye, and quite a journey," he said. "We have to outrun the wind itself. If we're not back before the gates close, none of this will matter."

'He's mad,' she thought. Lily reached to draw a curtain.

"Not yet," Jonquil said. "Not until we're at the outskirts of the city." Her uncle closed his eyes and his massive head sunk on his chest. "Now, I suggest you sleep before first light comes. We have a long trip ahead." Minutes later, Jonquil was snoring like air squeezing through a pair of bellows.

Lily listened to the horses clopping down the street. She waited until she was certain he was asleep and then peeked out of the curtains. They were in a part of the city she didn't know. Fish peddlers were setting up for the day. A night watchman made his rounds swinging a lantern in front of him. Newsboys unloaded bundles of papers from a cart. A man in an apron with a handlebar mustache swept in front of the Greasy Eel Tavern. They traveled down streets filthy with refuse and up grand boulevards where captains of industry slept on silk sheets. As her hand inched for the carriage door, one of Jonquil's eyes popped open and he said, "Don't try it, dove."

The sky seeped pink, then violet, then orange.

Weariness overtook her and she fell into an uneasy slumber. When she awoke, they were outside the city. Jonquil was watching her and eating wild boar jerky from a pack.

"Sleep well?" he said.

"I would have done better in my own bed," Lily snipped.

"As would I. Neither got their wish, though," her uncle said with a laugh.

"Where are we?" Lily pulled the curtain back and bright sunshine invaded the carriage. Farmland surrounded them on all sides. In the distance, she saw the jagged peaks of mountains capped with snow. She let the curtain fall back in place.

"Leave it open. You'll crave sunshine where we're going," Jonquil said.

Lily opened both windows and tied the drapes in place. The carriage rocketed along the road, bouncing so hard she thought her teeth were going to rattle out of her head.

"Is it safe to go this fast?" she asked, grabbing her seat for support.

"Probably not," Jonquil said. "But better to put distance between us and the city before your parents wake."

"They'll come after me," Lily said defiantly.

"They'd be wiser not to. Even as children, though, Thomas and Moira followed their hearts and not their minds."

They rode in silence, Lily staring at the passing

scenery and Jonquil chewing on jerky. In the sunlight, his skin was so white as to be translucent. The only color was the red around his lips.

"Why didn't my father tell us about you?" Lily asked.

"He probably hoped Deiva and I and Nightfall Gardens would go away like a bad dream. But there are some dreams from which you don't wake."

"Deiva… is my grandmother?" she said hesitantly.

"Aye. I wouldn't expect any motherly affection, though. She's hard enough to break stone, and the only thing she cares about is her dead husband and that cursed house."

"You said she was ill, that the darkness might escape if she dies. I… what does that mean?" Lily asked.

"Nothing wrong with your ears then," Jonquil said. "I wondered how much you and your brother heard listening at the grate."

"How did you… ?"

"You learn many things when shadows slip from dusk and your senses are all upon which you can rely. Enough questions for now; bask in the light, bones rarely warm where we go."

Jonquil didn't speak for many hours after that. Lily watched as farmland gave way to forest. The trees were so thick that branches scraped against the sides of the carriage. A family of deer dashed across the road and was enveloped by the woods.

By late afternoon, the trees had thinned and the mountains doubled in size ahead of them. Still, the carriage didn't slow. They passed over a wooden bridge so old and rickety that Lily's heart raced into her throat with fear it would collapse. When they were halfway across, Lily leaned out and saw a drop of several hundred feet to the river below. The carriage wheels were only inches from going over either side. Once they were across the gorge, the horses took off at a gallop again.

The day cooled and the sky flowered blue, then purple. Two villagers carrying baskets on their shoulders were the first people Lily saw that afternoon. Not long after, they traveled through a village of sagging, straw-roofed homes. Horses were drawn up in front of the local inn and the smell of frying duck and other meats wafted into the carriage as they passed. Lily's stomach grumbled, but they didn't slow. She looked at her uncle, shadows caging his face, to complain. Jonquil was staring out the window with such abject dejection that she said nothing.

The carriage stopped only when it became unsafe to continue in the darkness. "Mind yourself," Jonquil said as they stepped down to the muddy road. "These woods are full of creatures with sharp eyes and sharper teeth. I don't want to go stumbling around after you in the dark."

The two men driving the carriage collected firewood and soon a blaze was going. There was hardtack and apples to go around. Lily was going to protest, but instead, she ate her fill and felt even hungrier when she was finished. Her uncle edged close to the fire and flames danced in his eyes. He rubbed his hands together as if to begin a story.

"You have many questions," he started.

Lily felt the soreness of the day's ride in her back and shoulders. "Oh, you're talking to me now," she said, irritated.

Jonquil's men grunted laughter. Her uncle smiled. "Forgive me, niece, but I've spent too much time alone in the mist. A man grows odd when he has nothing but his own thoughts to keep him company."

"Who are these men?" She gestured to the cloaked figures next to her uncle. "Why do you wear coats made from wolves?"

"These are my most trusted advisors, Arfast and Skuld," Jonquil said and the men laughed again. "Introduce yourselves to my fair niece."

"I'm Arfast," the younger of the two said. He jumped to his feet and plucked a ball of fire from the air. He reached behind his back and pulled out a second ball of fire and started juggling. A third, fourth and fifth ball appeared and soon he was tossing them high in the air and in between his legs. Once he was finished, he caught the fireballs and they disappeared. He winked and bowed to Lily.

"Showoff," Skuld said. His voice was gravely and he was older than her uncle. "You'll have to excuse my companion, my lady. Life hasn't seasoned him yet." He threw his cloak over his shoulder and displayed the ragged stump that ended at the elbow. "You ask why we wear the cloaks. I wear mine to remind myself what a moment of carelessness can cost."

"And *I'm* the showoff," Arfast said. "He shows that bloody stump every chance he gets."

Lily thought Skuld might be angered by the young man's comment, but he chuckled. "You have guts, I'll give you that," Skuld said. "No sense, but lots of guts."

"These are defenders of Nightfall Gardens," Jonquil said. "When something slithers from the dusk, there is no one else you want at your side. Believe me on that."

"And what is Nightfall Gardens?"

Her uncle stared at the millions of stars ready to burst through the black sky overhead.

"I've wondered that same thing many times myself," he said, and a reverent tone crept into his voice. "It's our ancestral home, where Blackwoods have lived and died for centuries beyond memory. It's also a space that exists in-between. Dark is never far and is always looking for a way in. The women of our family have managed to it hold it back, though it has come in many disguises. If the darkness should ever escape from Nightfall Gardens, it will be set free upon the world. I dread what would happen then. That's why you must come back."

'Mad as three kinds of hatters,' Lily thought, but

said nothing. A wolf howled somewhere in the nearby mountains. Skuld grabbed an ax and slipped into the trees.

"Why must it be a Blackwood woman?" she asked.

"That's best heard from your grandmother," her uncle said. "Each Blackwood woman passes her knowledge on to the next before she slips into the shadowland."

"In other words, you don't know," Lily said.

Arfast was balancing a knife blade on the tip of his index finger. "She has you there," he said grinning.

"There are certain things only the female Blackwoods know," Jonquil said. "It has always been this way. If you'd seen what your father and I have, you wouldn't have any doubts."

"And what do the men do, while the women are 'defending against the darkness'?" she asked.

"We patrol the gardens and protect our people when something slips through," he said. "We're the watchers of the three gardens. We make sure nothing goes in or comes out of them."

"And if I refuse my duty?" Lily thrust her chin forward.

"Then heavens help us, you are the last of the Blackwood daughters."

'He really believes it,' she thought. *'They all do. It's no wonder my parents ran away.'*

Skuld came back shortly afterward emptyhanded. The three men slept on the ground with their cloaks as pillows. Lily made a bed of furs that were given to her. The woods pressed cold and empty on either side. The mountains were cutouts on the horizon. The fire died to embers.

She closed her eyes and fell into a deep sleep that was disturbed by a dream of her brother Silas. He was watching her. His eyes swirled blue and brown in the starlight. He reached for her, but before their hands could touch, something jarred her and she was awake. Jonquil was standing over her. It was still black as pitch, with no sign of the coming day.

"Rise and shine your highness. We have many leagues to go and time mocks us with the grains of sand that pour through its hourglass," he said.

Arfast and Skuld pushed the horses even harder that day. The carriage bounced so hard along the road Lily thought all the bones in her body would break. At one point, they struck a pothole and Jonquil banged his head, cursing out loud. Lily couldn't help smiling. Her uncle barred his teeth and growled.

She only tried to engage him in conversation once. "How did my father and mother meet? Why did they leave Nightfall Gardens?"

"Moira was of the people of the mist," Jonquil said. The rough edges fell from his face as he remembered. "She was the most beautiful girl, too beautiful for that place. One day, Thomas and I were —." He shook his head and caught himself. "To hell with it," he said. "I'm tired of answering your questions."

They came to the mountains in the early afternoon. The ground was rockier and steeper and rutted into a barely passable trail. The carriage climbed for the rest of the day. Skuld shouted at the horses and lashed them forward. Lily watched out the windows as the ground shrank further away until it felt she could see halfway across the world. The temperature dropped inside the carriage as the air thinned. Clouds drifted by, only feet above them. Pines grew thick along the ridge and the sweet smell of their needles filled the carriage. She saw a few stone huts along the way. Dirty children slipped from the homes and watched warily as they passed.

At sunset, the carriage struggled to the peak of the mountain and stopped so they could take in the majestic scene. The sun was the color of a ripe plum on the horizon while the sky was a thousand shades of reds and yellows. From here, Lily could see all the way to New Amsterdam. The famous city looked no larger than a matchbox. On the other side, the mountain dropped precipitously into a shaded valley through which a mighty river roared. Beyond that, other mountains trailed off into the frozen north.

"Fridgeir's Valley," Jonquil stroked his chin thoughtfully. "Another day's journey and we'll be home."

The carriage descended, rocks sliding out from under the wheels. More than once it seemed as though the horses were losing control and the carriage was going to plummet to the valley below. At the last minute, Skuld would restrain the horses, whipping them and shouting a string of obscenities that echoed off far mountain walls.

When they could no longer see the road, the drivers found a place where they could camp for the night. Arfast made a fire and once again they supped on hardtack and apples. Lily was hungrier than ever and growing angrier by the moment. She glared at her uncle with hatred. He was the one who had kidnapped her from her family. Because of him, she was hungry and her parents were worried. She was tired and covered in road dust and there was nowhere for her to run, except into these desolate mountains.

Jonquil caught his niece glowering at him. The ragged scar on his cheek shone in the firelight. "Yes, you definitely take after your mother," he said.

After dinner, Lily dragged her furs as far from the men as she could. Even through the furs, the ground was hard and rocky. A tree root pushed into her back. She rolled on her side and tried to rest. Sleep evaded her. The fire burned to coals. Stars shimmered through the lime-green band of the Northern Lights overhead. She imagined herself performing on the great stages of the world, jaunting from party to party, heralded in the press as the greatest actress of her time. She would wear pearls, diamonds and expensive gowns. No more hand-me-downs that her mother stitched together. There would be handsome princes and sheiks who courted her. Everything happening now would be a bad dream.

The sound of something moving softly in the dark brought Lily out of her fantasy. She heard crunching rocks and feet padding near the carriage. She sat up and stared into the dark. The sound was gone now, if it had ever been there at all. She looked where the men slept. Jonquil and Skuld were spread out near the remains of fire. Where was Arfast?

At that moment, Lily heard a commotion from the woods and Arfast yelled, "Got you!" Jonquil and Skuld stirred. Lily climbed to her feet. The guardsman pushed a lanky boy in to the clearing. She couldn't make out his features in the dark.

"Caught us a live one," Arfast said. He threw the boy to his knees in front of Jonquil and Skuld.

In the glow of the fading firelight there was no mistaking who it was.

"Silas!" Lily said, running to her brother.

4

Song of the Pans

When Silas saw Jonquil abducting his sister, he raced to the prop room and down into the tunnels. A plan was already forming in his mind. He followed one of the passages to the sewer that ran below the street. Water dripped from the ceiling. Fungus glowed in the dark on the walls. The fetid smell made him gag. He tried not to think of the rat, big as a dog, that had stood on its hind legs and chittered at him the last time he was there. An iron ladder, thick with rust, led to the street above. Silas scrambled up it, afraid they would already be gone or that he had misjudged where he would come out. He pushed the manhole cover out of the way and was relieved to see he was directly below the carriage. Voices came from the front where the horses were. "Poor girl has no idea what awaits her," a leathery sounding man said. "That's why

Jonquil isn't giving her a choice in whether she comes or not," a younger sounding man replied.

Silas crawled over cobblestones and out behind the carriage. A ladder led to the roof where Lily's trunk was. He climbed it, careful to make as little noise as possible. Once he was on the roof, he crept to the trunk and popped the latch, afraid it would make a noise loud enough to draw attention. Below, he saw two men wearing the same kind of coat as his uncle. They cinched the horses, making sure all was ready for the trip. "A real tragedy, but it always has been for Blackwoods," the older man said. Silas opened the trunk carefully and climbed on top of her clothes, pulling the lid after him so it was only open an inch.

For two days, he jounced and jostled as the carriage raced through farmland and climbed into the mountains. Silas was curled in the trunk, his long legs up under his chin. Every so often he cracked the lid and peeked at the passing countryside. *'Where are they taking her?'* he thought. Then, *'How do we get out of here?'*

On the first night, he snuck out of the trunk well after everyone was asleep and crept to the woods where he could relieve himself. Mountain surrounded him on every side. The forest was louder with creatures than a city intersection busy with people. *'We wouldn't make it far in there,'* he thought. On the way back, Lily opened her eyes as he passed. He froze on the spot and waited. His sister stared for a moment longer, closed her eyes and went back to sleep.

The carriage ascended to the top of the mountain the next day. Silas felt its wheels sliding under them as they went higher. He could hear the older man whipping the horses onward and cursing a blue streak as he bounced inside the trunk. They reached the mountain's peak near sunset. After a short rest, the carriage continued its journey, this time going down the other side of the mountain. Silas tried to remember the geography lessons his mother taught them. If he was right, these were the Fangfir Mountains or the gateway to the north. They were supposed to be haunted. The few people who lived there were a superstitious lot who wore talismans to protect from the Evil Eye. It was rumored that some of the people still worshipped the old animal gods. There was supposed to be a tribe of headless people who lived in the shadows of the mountains. Silas had read a newspaper story about a farmer at the foot of the Fangfirs who claimed to have been put under a spell and slept more than 100 years. The drawing with the story showed a wizened man with a beard stretching to his knees, blinking in sunlight. Travelers passing here were regularly robbed or found murdered. *And this is where our mother and father are from,'* Silas thought.

After everyone was asleep, Silas climbed down from the carriage. He moved slowly, careful to make as little noise as possible. Jonquil and his men slept close to the glowing embers of the fire. Lily was further away, by herself. His stomach growled and he clutched it with his hand as though he could quiet it down. The air was thin and crisp as he stepped into the trees. *'There'll be food and a comfortable bed at the end of all this,'* he thought.

A branch snapped behind him and a hand, hard as steel, clamped his neck. "Nice night for a walk, eh boy?" the young man said, wrenching Silas's arm behind his back. "No reason to be shy. We love company."

He was propelled towards the campfire. Jonquil and his other man were waiting with weapons drawn. Lily was the first to see him. "Silas!" she said. "Oh Silas, how did you get here!" Before anyone could stop her, she ran and embraced him.

"It's a bedraggled mountain rat," the older man said, clutching the ax that they used for cutting firewood in his one good arm. Jonquil stared grimly at the boy in front of him. "I'm afraid it's worse than some nighttime thief, this is my nephew. How did you find your way here? Are there others with you? Tell me now!" Their uncle's face was a raging torrent of anger.

"I — I hid in the trunk," Silas said and told his story of the last two days.

"Very dangerous," Jonquil said. He spit in the dirt. "You thought you could spirit your sister away from men of the dusk? It was a fool's errand."

"What other choice was there?" Silas asked. "To leave my sister to people I don't know?"

"Walk away and trust she can take care of herself," he said. "This isn't a children's game. There are dark forces at work here. Now, leave me to think," Jonquil turned to walk away.

Lily cleared her throat. "Wouldn't it be better if he came along? If I'm going to take over Nightfall Gardens, I'll need people I can trust."

Jonquil stopped. "What you say is true, but Nightfall Gardens cares nothing for Blackwood men, only the women. It's a hard life for the dusk riders, and that's exactly what your brother would become. It's always been that way."

"I'm not afraid," Silas said.

"You say that now lad, but wait until the Smiling Ladies try to kiss you, or you're lost in the Labyrinth with nothing but the starless night as a companion. Only an idiot wouldn't be frightened," Jonquil said. He and his men crouched by the fire to discuss what they were going to do with the boy.

"It was very foolish what you did," Lily said when the two were alone, though secretly she was pleased. "Do you think mother and father are coming after us?"

"As quickly as they can," Silas said. "I wouldn't be surprised if they catch up with us before Nightfall Gardens."

"What will happen then?" Lily asked.

"I don't know," Silas said truthfully. He thought of his parents battling the three men from the north and shuddered.

Their uncle came over. He had pulled the wolf

cloak tight about him and its jaws full of teeth seemed alive. "We'll take you as far as Eyum and then you must go back. We won't be responsible after that."

"No!" Lily shouted.

"I can take care of myself," Silas said.

"No doubt you can, but if you knew where you were going — " Jonquil said to Silas, then pointed at Lily " — and if you knew what you were asking of your brother, neither of you would be in such a rush to ask for the sacrifice."

There was no more sleep that night. Arfast and Skuld covered the fire and erased all signs that they had been there, while the others loaded the carriage. Silas rode with his sister inside as the carriage inched down the mountain in the darkness.

"We should be in Eyum by afternoon. Then you can put this behind you, boy, like your father and mother. Forget that any such place as the Gardens exists," Jonquil said.

"And Lily?" Silas asked. His sister was ghostly in the moonlight coming through the open carriage windows.

"She has no choice," their uncle said. "Best for each of you to forget the other exists."

Dawn came hours later. The sky lightened imperceptibly, until Silas could see the trees and valley that loomed in the distance.

The three traveled in silence. Silas turned plots in his head to save his sister, but all of them ended in defeat. Lily's brow furrowed as she daydreamed about standing ovations and roses thrown at her feet. Jonquil brooded more deeply the closer they came to home.

The road was little more than a washed-out rut at the bottom of the mountain. They saw no signs of life until they came upon an overturned carriage shortly before noon. It was a mail wagon used to deliver parcels from one end of the land to the other. Bags of mail were ripped open and envelopes blew in the grass at the side of the road.

Arfast stopped the carriage and jumped down. He looked into the wagon and studied the nearby ground. "No one's here," he said. "I see blood stains on the seat."

"Bandits," Jonquil muttered.

"What did they do with the driver?" Lily asked.

"Probably dragged him into the woods and killed him," their uncle said.

The words chilled Silas and his sister. Days ago, the worst thing that they worried about was Celeus Talbot falling off the stage drunk. They were crossing into a land that neither had ever imagined.

The uneasy feeling only grew stronger as they approached Eyum. The houses in the village were made from the slate that was found in abundance in the valley. A stone church with a crooked spire and a graveyard that was hundreds of years old were the centerpiece of the town. They only saw one person, a farmer's wife, leading two sickly cows down the road. She pitched a sign to ward against the Evil Eye when they passed. Silas noticed black crosses painted in charcoal on many of the doors.

"What are those for?" he asked.

Jonquil stared at him. "Those are houses that have been struck with the plague."

Silas felt a lump in his throat. It was decades since the Great Plague had struck New Amsterdam and other cities and brought them to their knees, but no one had forgotten. One in every three people was afflicted; most of those died, raving of madness and burning with thirst.

"I thought it had been wiped out?" Lily said.

"Many things that shouldn't be exist the closer we come to our ancestral home. This is spoiled land," their uncle said.

"You won't leave me here?" Silas said. Panic overtook him as he remembered that Jonquil had said this town would be his final stop.

"I'm not that cruel, lad." Jonquil tapped twice on the carriage ceiling. The horses picked up pace and soon the town was behind them. "We'll leave you at Mad Finnegan's near Nightfall Gardens. He'll have a bed to spare until your parents come looking."

Evening fell early in the valley. Shadows stretched across the mountain floor as they made their way deeper into the woods. White-capped mountains loomed in front of them as they bumped down the rocky trail. Jonquil pulled a blunderbuss from under his cloak and watched more closely out the windows.

"What do you see?" Silas asked. He and Lily leaned forward to look at the road going past.

"Maybe nothing, maybe something. Either way, I'd pull my head back, if you don't want it taken off," he said.

The carriage began to slow. Arfast called back. "A tree's fallen across the road!"

Jonquil's lips twitched in a thin smile. The wolf eyes glowed in the dusk. "Take these," he said, handing over a pair of blades that looked sharp enough to cut air. They were heavy in Silas's hand. He handed one to his sister.

"I don't know how to use this," Lily said. She switched the knife from hand to hand as though it were distasteful.

"You'll learn soon enough if a marauder breaks in here," Jonquil said. He opened the door. "You're Blackwoods. Act like it."

Silas leaned out and watched Arfast and Skuld trying to move the tree that was blocking them from passing.

"What is this then?" Jonquil said as he approached his men.

"Someone chopped it down on purpose," Skuld said. "I don't like it one bit."

"You don't like much, do you old man?" Arfast joked as the two lifted the tree and dragged it out of the way.

"What's happening?" Lily asked.

Silas was about to answer when he saw a flash

of red in the trees and marauders sprang from the woods and attacked the carriage. There were a dozen of them, dressed in rags and wielding rusty swords and antique pistols.

One of the men charged Jonquil. In the fading light of day Silas swore he could see twisting ram's horns on the man's forehead. His uncle pulled the trigger on the blunderbuss and the bandit's head disintegrated in a cloud of smoke.

Lily screamed at the sound of the weapon firing and dropped the knife to the floor. The door of the carriage ripped open and a bandit with a goat face peered at them and smiled. He was covered in course hair and his eyes were golden. Pointed nubs of horns rode above his devilish eyebrows. A red bandana was tied around his neck.

"Well, well, what do we have here?" he sniffed the air with his pointed snout. "Blackwoods, I reckon."

He reached in and grabbed Silas, who was frozen with fear. "I'll be back to play a sweet song for you on my flute," the goat man said bowing to Lily. "As soon as I finish with this stripling."

Silas was thrown from the carriage, and the air was knocked from him when he struck the ground. The battle raged all around. He saw Arfast fighting three goat men, swinging a sword and driving them toward the woods. Jonquil traded blows with a creature that stood seven foot tall and was encased in brown fur with horns the size of truncheons. There were humans as well. Skuld was hacking at the wooden shield of one of the goat creatures when a filthy man with matted hair stepped from the trees with a bow and arrow. Silas tried to warn him,but his lungs burned as he drew breath. The bandit notched an arrow and shot Skuld in the shoulder. His uncle's man bellowed, lashing out, and bringing his ax down on the goat creature before attacking the archer who was notching another arrow.

"Why so pale and wan?" the goat man from the carriage said. He leaned over Silas with a jewel-encrusted razor in his hand and light reflected from its wicked surface. His voice was melodic and Silas imagined the goat man must have a beautiful singing voice. Silas felt for the knife Jonquil had given him but it was lost when he was tossed from the carriage. The goat man leaned over him. He smelt of fresh summer days and hidden springs. The razor pressed against Silas's throat. "Don't worry. I'll give you a permanent grin so you're always happy!"

At that moment, the goat man's mouth dropped open in a wide O and he arched his back as a knife blade came out the front of his chest. The razor slid from his hand and he collapsed next to Silas.

Lily stood over her brother. Her blue dress was splattered in blood. She clutched Jonquil's knife. "He was going to hurt you," she said in shock.

The tide of battle turned in their favor. Arfast charged the goat men, slashing like a man possessed. Jonquil reloaded his blunderbuss and leveled a round at the nearest grotesquerie. Skuld waded through them with his battle-ax. The remaining goat men bounded back into the woods, leaving their dead and fallen behind.

"This one won't bother you again." Arfast said, nudging the body of the goat man with the red bandana.

Lily's eyes were troubled as she turned from the creature she killed.

"What are they?" Silas asked. Blood beaded on his neck where the razor had touched him. He didn't care to think about what would've happened if the goat man pressed harder.

"Pans. They came from the Labyrinth in the Gardens," Jonquil said. He pulled the blade from the goat man's back with a sucking sound and wiped it on his pant leg. "They escaped through the gate years ago and have caused misery for travelers ever since."

"Why not run away from here?" Silas asked. Half a dozen bodies were strewn about the road. Skuld walked among them to see if any still held the breath of life.

"The Gardens draw them and will not let go," Jonquil said. "They can't bear to be too far from the possibility of what exists there."

"Enough dawdling. More will come if we wait much longer," Skuld said. He drank from a flagon of red wine that he pulled from his cloak. When he was finished, he scratched the stump of his right arm. "Wretched thing always itches after a battle."

Silas helped Arfast and Skuld drag the bodies of the dead to the woods. The road lay clear ahead of them again.

"Ride on top and keep your eyes open for danger," Jonquil said to Silas. "The Pans are vengeful and won't forget what happened today." His uncle went to tend to Skuld's wound.

Silas stopped Lily as she climbed into the carriage. Her face held an expression like a sleepwalker who believes they are dreaming.

"I've never killed anything larger than a cockroach in my life," Lily said. There were swollen circles under her eyes.

"You did it to save me," Silas said. "Don't trouble yourself on this."

"Those things couldn't have been real," Lily said. "What if there are more monsters like this at Nightfall Gardens? I can't go there alone."

"You won't be alone," Silas said.

For the next two hours he rode on top of the carriage, scanning the woods for glimpses of the Pans. Twilight came and they crossed a river that was swollen with water from recent storms. As the carriage started to climb into the mountains again, he caught his first glimpse of Nightfall Gardens. There was nothing else it could be.

The ancient-looking palace rose out of nowhere to dominate the landscape. It was protected by a high stone wall that stretched to the horizon. He saw a jumble of towers, spires, and walls of windows that soared toward the heavens. Statues of gargoyles dominated the eaves. Gaslight flickered on either side of the entry. Nightfall Gardens seemed to grow larger and smaller as Silas watched, as though it were breathing like a living thing. *'I can feel its presence from here,'* he thought.

"Home," Arfast spit out as though it were poison on his tongue. He turned to look at Silas. "Pray this is as close as you ever come to it, boy."

Silas lost track of the mansion as the road curved. A harvest moon appeared over the mountains guiding their way. Soon, they came to a dilapidated inn. Chickens played in the yard and smoke curled from the chimney. No horses or people were anywhere in sight. Their carriage came to a stop. Jonquil climbed out as the tavern keep appeared. Silas gasped when he saw him. The man's face, neck and arms were tattooed with strange hieroglyphs of jackal-faced men, pharaohs and pyramids.

"Finnegan!" Jonquil exclaimed, grabbing his friend in a bear hug.

"Come to drink with the damned?" his friend said, laughing.

"You're too nimble for the old god," Jonquil said. "You'll slip through his net yet."

"None do," Finnegan said. "But at least I live with true love in the meanwhile."

A woman, dark and beautiful and mysterious, came out of the inn. "Hello Jonquil. I wondered what all this noise was. I hoped it wasn't my husband talking to the chickens again." She smiled.

"They're better conversation than you think," Finnegan said. "So to what do we owe this pleasure?"

"Hello, Amunet," Jonquil said to the wife. "Perhaps I can talk with the two of you alone for a moment." He put his arm around their shoulders and steered them back into the inn.

"Why does he have those tattoos?" Silas asked.

"Markings," Skuld said. "So Osiris, the god of death, can track him."

Arfast chuckled. "Mad Finnegan did something that's only been accomplished a few times in the history of the world."

"What?" Silas asked.

"He stole something belonging to a god. Amunet, Finnegan's wife, died of the shaking fever shortly after they were married. The poor man went wild with grief and journeyed into the White Garden, until he brought her back. They left Nightfall Gardens so Osiris couldn't find them. The old god's been angry ever since."

'They must be mad,' Silas thought. *'Yet, I've seen things today I don't know how to explain.'* He hung over the side of the carriage and peered in at his sister. Lily was clutching her hands and biting her lower lip. A pensive look was on her face.

"Perhaps you should stay. I would feel awful if anything happened to you," she said.

"We're in this together. At least until mother and father rescue us." He tried to smile.

"*If* they are able to rescue us," Lily said. She

looked up at him.

Jonquil came back with Finnegan and Amunet. "It's settled then," he said, pulling his cloak tight about him. "You'll stay here until your parents arrive."

Silas dropped to the ground. "No," he said. "I'm going with you."

"Don't start this again, lad. Your mother and father are already losing one child."

"They are losing no one. I'm coming along," he said.

"You're weak," Jonquil said. "You'll do no one any favors, only put us in danger."

"You can train me," he said. "I won't leave Lily."

His uncle took a threatening step toward him. "This is no life of fine feather beds and warm summer sunshine. You'll lose the light, you'll lose all you've known and you'll probably lose your life."

"I don't care. I'm coming," Silas said.

A horn blew in the woods.

"Pans," Skuld said.

"We have to go," Arfast said, unsheathing his sword.

"Blast it all," Jonquil spit in the dirt. "I'm sorry Finnegan, Amunet. We've brought trouble down on your house."

"Don't worry about the wee goaties," Finnegan said. "I have a couple of muskets that will take the fight from them."

Jonquil sighed. "Get in the carriage then, boy. And never forget you do this of your own free will."

"I won't," Silas said.

The carriage rumbled down the road minutes later. The moon loomed larger on the horizon, one moment appearing yellow and the next red through a trick of the light. Skuld pushed the horses as they entered the final miles to the house. Silas watched out the window as Nightfall Gardens came into view again. The house was heavy with the weight of its own existence. It shifted and moved as he watched.

"Somebody's following us." Jonquil stared out the other window.

Silas looked back and saw two horses charging down the road. Their riders were bent forward, cloaks flapping with the wind. They were only pinpricks but he could already tell who they were.

"Mother, Father!" he said.

Lily pushed him out of the way. "Where? What are you talking about?"

Silas pointed. "They're coming!"

"Your parents never had the sense God gave a goose," Jonquil said. He rapped twice on the carriage roof and it jolted forward.

Nightfall Gardens was ahead of them now. A grand promenade of dead trees led to a black gate tipped with spikes. A stone wall crumbling with age surrounded the property. Silas and Lily had never seen a house so large and foreboding in their lives.

"The gate's closing," Silas said.

"What?" Jonquil turned from watching Thomas and Moira. The riders were coming up on them fast.

"The gate's closing," Silas repeated again.

Jonquil looked. The two gates leading to Nightfall Gardens were coming together. "No!" he shouted. "It's too soon." Skuld must have seen the same thing, because the horses went even faster. The carriage was rumbling so hard it felt as though it was coming undone.

"They're going to catch us," Lily said. For the first time since the journey had started there was eagerness in her voice.

Their parents were so close Silas could see the grim determination etched on their faces and the froth on their horses' mouths as they drew closer. He glanced in the other direction and saw that the gates were halfway closed. Skulls made from stone, smoothed by centuries of rain, guarded either side of the entrance.

"Hang on," Jonquil yelled as the carriage struck the closing gates. There was a maddening scraping sound. Lily and Silas were pitched to the floor and the carriage went up on two wheels and slammed down as it passed on to the grounds before grinding to a halt. Silas made it to a window in time to see his parents charging at the gates as they slammed shut. One second Moira and Thomas were there, and then there was a flash of a light that blinded him. When Silas opened his eyes, his parents were gone and nothingness existed on the other side of the gates. It was only then that he realized Lily was watching the whole thing over his shoulder.

Jonquil straightened his cloak and smiled unpleasantly.

"Welcome to Nightfall Gardens," he said.

5
Most Cursed of the Cursed

Wolves howled in the creeping mist as the carriage rattled to Nightfall Gardens. The moon was blood red and so large it threatened to swallow the house. *'Everything's darker here,'* Lily thought. She put her arm out the window and the night was so thick and gloomy that it seemed to have actual weight.

"You'll get used to it," Jonquil said. They were his first words since the gates closed minutes before. "It's always dusk or dark here, but to a Blackwood that spells home."

"What happened to our parents? To the world outside the gate?" Silas asked. He was looking back toward the entrance. An impenetrable whiteness existed on the other side of the wall.

"The gates only open on the world a few days every year," he said. "Your parents are trapped outside and we're trapped inside. Now, enough questions, Deiva can explain the rest."

The carriage pulled to a stop in front of the entrance. The house stretched as far as the eye could see in all directions. Parts of Nightfall Gardens seemed thousands of years old, others looked like they'd been built yesterday. Winged gargoyles guarded the doors and roof.

Lily climbed down from the carriage. She glanced up at a candlelit window and thought she saw a hunched figure pull away. Curling fingers of fog blew across the grounds. Hundreds of fragrant night-blooming flowers grew in a nearby garden.

"Dragon flowers for protection," Jonquil said. "The first lesson for both of you is never walk in the Gardens at full dark. The Smiling Ladies and others are about that would do you harm."

The front door creaked open and a woman with skin the color of a slug stood there holding a candle. She was bald and her eyes were white with no pupils. Her skin oozed, leaving wet tracks on her maid's uniform. She gave a toothless grin on seeing Jonquil.

"Didn't think we'd be seeing you again so soon, Mr. Jonquil. Close one, that was," she gurgled.

"You won't get rid of me that easy, Polly," he said.

"Why this must be Miss Lily. Bless my heart if she isn't the spitting image of Miss Moira," the maid said. "And I'm as dumb as a grub worm if Master Silas here doesn't look just like his father." She glanced into the dark. "Where are my manners? Come in, come in. There are nasty things about right now."

Lily thought she felt the house move under her as she entered. Silas stayed close by her side. Jonquil followed behind them. Polly glided along in front, leaving a glistening trail on the floor. "Miss Deiva will be happy to see you, she will," the maid oozed.

The grand entrance of the house had fallen on hard times. Torn tapestries displaying images of past Blackwoods covered grimy walls. Moldings were coming undone. Cobwebs filled the corners of what must have once been an impressive room. A majestic chandelier glinting yellow could have used a good dusting. Lily gasped when she looked at it. Displayed in each of its hundreds of crystals, she saw tiny screaming faces calling for help.

"Look," she said grabbing Silas by the arm.

"What?" her brother replied.

Lily pointed towards the chandelier but there was nothing there. "I could have sworn —."

Polly made a wet giggle. "Oh, there are many tricks of the eye here. Many tricks indeed."

They followed her up a winding staircase. The candle cast the only light, and darkness poured from the walls, a moving liquid that sucked at the tiny flame she carried.

"How is she?" Jonquil asked.

"Still won't leave the room," Polly said. "Says Abigail visits her in the witching time."

"Nonsense," Jonquil said.

"That's what I told her. Told her it was only in her head, I did," Polly said. She glided along the carpeted corridor. The candle was held far in front of her as if she were afraid the flame would get close and sizzle her skin. "Miss Abigail's been gone these many years, I said."

The candle sputtered as they came to another hallway. Lily heard what sounded like children's voices whispering beneath one of the doors. "*Come in, come in and play with us,*" the voices said. From behind a different door someone was crying. "*Please, no more. I can't take any more.*" Silas grabbed her hand and squeezed. She could feel him shaking with fear. Polly and Jonquil continued their conversations as though the sounds were no more than flies buzzing on the wall.

"So, what news from the Gardens?" Jonquil asked.

"Terrible, terrible," Polly said with a shake of her gelatinous head. "Ill omens are everywhere. Wolves were caught trying to sneak into the Labyrinth and Shadow Garden. No one knows why. A family from Priortage was found with the life drained out of them. The Gardens are restless, and it's taking all your men to hold back what lives inside."

"It's worse than I thought," Jonquil said.

"Dark days. Dark days indeed. But now Miss Lily is here. I wouldn't worry about it too much," the maid said.

They came to a rounded door at the end of the

hall. Polly banged three times. For a moment there was no answer, and then the clipped tones of a highborn woman responded. "Come in and be quick about it."

Lily didn't know what she expected her grandmother to look like, but it wasn't the woman sitting in the chair by the window. Deiva was dressed all in black, with a veil covering her face. Her hands were the only part of her that could be seen and they were so white as to be lifeless.

"Why do you come so late at night?" Deiva asked Polly. "Didn't I tell you I wanted no visitors?"

"Begging your pardon, Miss, but your son has returned with your grandchildren," Polly said.

"Thomas? Thomas is here?" Deiva said, showing a spark of interest.

"No Miss. Your other son, Jonquil," Polly said.

"Oh," Deiva slumped in her chair. "Bring them forward if you must, but be careful not to disturb anything."

'She lives in the past,' Lily thought. A table was set for two in part of the room, but the food had long moldered. The white tablecloth was brown with age. A man's belongings were everywhere: a hunting jacket hung over a chair, a pipe filled with tobacco set next to an ashtray. A cabinet filled with ancient weapons was open in a corner. Dust covered everything as though the room hadn't been aired out in decades.

"I'll leave you to it. Ring the bell if you need

anything," Polly said. She slid up to Lily and Silas. "I'm so glad you're home. I could just eat you up, I could." The maid squeezed them on the cheeks. Her fingers squelched against their skin and left slime on their faces.

Lily started to recoil in disgust but decided that would be bad manners. When the maid was gone, she and Silas scrubbed their cheeks.

"Well, let me see them," Deiva said. "Your father will be home any time now and I have to be ready for him."

"Mother, Father is never —," Jonquil started.

"Enough!" Deiva said, her veil fluttering. "He'll be coming from the Gardens soon and then it's time for dinner. Let me see what Thomas has been doing while you've been wasting your time chasing hobgoblins in the petunias."

Jonquil gritted his teeth and nudged the children forward. Their grandmother straightened her dress with her toadstool-colored hands. Every so often she glanced out the windows as though expecting someone to arrive.

"Who do we have here?" she said as Lily and Silas approached. "Come to your grandmother."

Lily smelled the sickly scent of something rotting. Intense eyes examined her through the black veil. Deiva placed an icy hand on her face, turning it from one side to the other. "Hmmm. You look exactly like your mother. Let's hope you don't have her arrogant attitude. What's your name, child?"

"Lily, Grandmother. I only hope I take after my mother and not *other* members of the family," Lily said trembling with rage.

Deiva laughed, the sound like water pumping from a rusty well. "Too true, too true. Many lilies grow here in Nightfall Gardens. They protect from evil and witches and are the flower that fairies sup. Let's hope you're rightly named, for Blackwood women are the most cursed of the cursed."

Their grandmother turned to look out the window as though afraid of missing something that might come out of the fog that obscured the gardens. When she was certain the grounds were empty, she scrutinized Silas.

"I see your father in you and also my Great Uncle Octavius. His eyes were the same as yours. There was always a merry twinkle about him and song on his lips but he forgot an important rule: Never trust the Gardens. He lay down for a nap without noticing the Bleeding Heart roots that were hidden nearby. When he awakened, the roots were peeling his skin like a blade peels a potato. We heard his screams all the way from the house. By the time they freed him, he was nothing but a bloody lump of muscle. He never again forgot where he was after that. I hope you'll be more careful."

The house creaked and groaned. Light rain pattered against the window. Lily's jaw dropped with surprise as the room doubled in length before her eyes. *'That can't be possible,'* she thought. But did anything in the last few days make sense?

"I'm sure you have many questions," Deiva said. "I've been outside of the Gardens in your world. I know how different it is. It's our burden to be Blackwoods, though, and that means never being at ease."

"Why?" Lily asked. *'My poor mad grandmother may have settled herself long ago to this fate, but the great stages in Paris are calling to me and I won't be satisfied until I'm upon them.'*

The old woman gave one last longing look out the window and trundled to a shelf where she removed an ancient leather book. Deiva's black dress dragged the floor. The train was covered in filth.

"It's in here, all of it," she said. "The story of how our family became the most damned in the history of the human race. How we ended up caretakers of Nightfall Gardens and why when the last female Blackwood dies, the Gardens will open and everything foul, noxious, and evil will spill out and signal the last days."

Deiva thumbed through the book as she talked. The parchment-like pages were so brittle that they looked as though they might crumble and blow away. The letters were written in an archaic script Lily had never seen before.

"The fall of our family makes for rich reading if you understand old speak," their grandmother said.

"Tell us, then," Lily said. The long journey, the

nightmare of Nightfall Gardens, all of it was wearing on her.

"Patience my dear. You'll learn that trait here. Time is all one has in this place," Deiva said. "Would you like to know about the first Blackwood then?"

"I've already told you I would," Lily snapped.

Their grandmother laughed again. "Indeed, you did. Take a seat then," Deiva turned to their uncle. "For the gods' sake, Jonquil, sit down. You're making me nervous."

Jonquil rubbed his hands anxiously on his cloak. *'He's out of his element,'* Lily thought. *'But why should that be? This is his home.'*

Lily and Silas sat next to their grandmother at the window. The rain tapped softly against glass. The smell of sickness radiating from her was overwhelming. Deiva reached under her veil and scratched her face. Lily heard something burst and leaned away from her.

"Ahh, itches like the dickens. Now where was I? Oh yes, the first Blackwood. I suppose she wasn't so different from the generations that came after. Little did she know one moment of curiosity would doom us all — but those are the rules the old gods play by."

Thunder and lightning crashed outside the window where the heavy fog met the gardens and jarred the candles on the table. Mad shadows danced upon the walls.

"These were the first days when strange beasts

rode upon the waves and people were fearful to go out at night for what lurked in the forest. Old gods walked in human disguise. Dragons ruled the air and the dark was controlled by the undead. It was a time of sadness and fear. Evil blanketed the land and no place was safe. The first humans were hunted and killed almost to extinction."

Lily felt gooseflesh prickle on her skin. Nightfall Gardens was oddly quiet. Jonquil shifted in his chair as though he couldn't find a comfortable spot.

"But as there was bad, there was good," Deiva continued. "And one of the old gods, Prometheus, took pity on humankind. He forged a box from the very fires of the earth that could contain the wickedness of the world. He trapped that evil inside the box and locked it so at last there was paradise. Without their enemies, humans multiplied and there came a time when people forgot how it had been. The old stories faded from memory and became nothing more than fairytales told over campfires, until they were so distorted that there was little truth left in them."

The moon was gone now. Thunderstorms rushed across the sky. Lightening flashed green deep within a cloud. Deiva pressed her face against the glass as the rain started pouring. "Do you think he'll be safe out there?" she said. "He and his men should be home anytime now."

"Mother," Jonquil said gently.

"No, you're right. He'll be safe and I must continue the tale."

"You said that the old gods died," Silas said.

"Well, yes and no. Some died and some were locked in Prometheus's box. They were none too happy about that either. Be that as it may, one afternoon many years ago, a young woman named Pandora discovered a man raging with fever by her family's well."

Deiva opened the book and began reading from the ancient pages:

He must have been handsome when he was younger, Pandora thought. The man's hair ran to his shoulders and his eyes blazed golden. He was dressed in beggar's garb and carried a rucksack that had seen ten thousand miles.

"Are you sick?" she asked.

"Of all but life and a taste of water for my lips," he said.

Pandora filled a dipper and he drank heartily. When he was finished, the man lay back and closed his eyes. It was then that she noticed how ill he really was. She put a hand against his forehead and felt the fire burning within.

"We must get you back to the house," she said.

"Nay," the man said. "Let me die here in the sun."

"You mustn't talk that way. There's a healing woman in the village. I can run and fetch her."

The man smiled wearily. "I would be gone by the time you came back and besides, there's nothing to fear in death."

Pandora was young, though, and death terrified her.

"Don't worry, child," the man said. "I have lived

longer than most. What's your name?"

"Pandora," she said.

"Mine is Prometheus," he said. "I ask only one favor of you."

"Name it and it shall be done."

"There is a box within my travelling satchel. When I am gone, I want you to drop it deep in the well and never say a word about it."

Pandora nodded.

"You must promise me that you'll never open it, for what's inside spells ruin for all," he said.

"I promise," Pandora said.

"Good child," he said.

Prometheus began raving about the old gods Zeus and Hera and the creatures of the night such as demons, succubi and ghouls. He talked until his throat was raw about those evils waiting for their chance to destroy humankind.

Night came. Prometheus grew quiet. His heaving chest gave the only sign that he was still alive. Pandora opened his rucksack and found the box. It was made of a heavy dark wood and scorched with the imprint of fire. She turned the box in her hands and thought she heard gold coins jingle. 'What if there's treasure inside?' she thought. Did she really know who Prometheus was? He might be one of those mad misers that lived like a pauper with chest full of rubies hoarded in their yard. The box was beautiful, after all. Why would he want her to throw it away and not give it to her? The longer she held the box, the more jealousy tore at her heart. Finally, she could contain herself no longer. 'It's mine,' Pandora thought. She searched frantically through the bag until she found a silver key.

Prometheus slept quietly now. His face was waxen and only a little pulse beat in his brow.

'He was delirious. He would want me to have it,' Pandora thought. The madness overtook her and she turned the key in the lock. The lid exploded open and a black cloud poured forth from the box. Pandora screamed as every evil that had ever existed began swarming out of the box and covering the earth.

"No," she screamed, realizing what she'd done.

The lid slammed shut in her hands and Prometheus stood in front of her, his eyes burning with fury. "Do you know what you did?"

"Nuh – No. I only wanted to see what was inside," Pandora stammered.

"You promised," he said "Because of you, who knows what terrors have escaped into the world."

With the last of his strength, the old god captured those dark beings that had escaped and carved an in-between place where all the terrors of the world could dwell. Prometheus realized humanity would never be safe while the box was around, so he buried it deep within the gardens of this new place. As punishment for her broken promise, he made Pandora and her family the gatekeepers that would watch over it until the last female of their line died. Their curse in life to make sure all the wicked and dark things locked up in the gardens would never be free to torment humanity again. When the last female dies the end days will be signaled.

Deiva closed the book. Candles sputtered and

flickered around the room. Cold pressed against Lily. Dampness filled the air and she wished for a thick blanket to cover herself from the dank air. The rain continued beating its fingers against the glass. Their grandmother was quiet for a moment, her face hidden behind the veil.

"Pandora was the first Blackwood," Deiva said. "A hundred generations have been cursed to this place because of her moment of weakness. So much for the gods being merciful."

"But I don't understand," Lily said. "What's to keep us from leaving and letting this whole place fall to the ground?"

"Absolutely nothing. Many times I've come close to it as well. But the evil that exists here, the threat of it being freed and what it would do keeps me here as it did my mother and her mother going back to the start of time."

Lily felt a great rage. She didn't want anything to do with this place. She wanted carriage doors opened for her and dinner at the finest restaurants in Paris. Applause and adoration were what she craved. Not life in this horrible, horrible place. "I didn't ask for this!" she said.

"Neither did I, yet here we are," Deiva said.

"I want to go home," Lily said. "Nightfall Gardens will take care of itself."

"Even if we let you, you couldn't leave now," her grandmother said.

"Why?"

"Because the gate only opens once a year and

after it's closed no one can come or leave," Deiva said.

"We rode in the gates. We could also ride out of them," Lily said stubbornly.

"If you managed to make it through them or over the wall, you would find nothing on the other side. Do you think you're the first to think of this? Every Blackwood who has tried has never been heard from again," Deiva told her.

Lily fumed and crossed her arms. *'If there's a way out of here, I'll find it,'* she thought.

Jonquil stood, wiping his hands on his jerkin. "Come on, lad. It won't be long before the cock crows and you'll need strength to start your new job."

"New job?" Silas said.

"Aye, you'll stay with me and the other men in the bunkhouse. In the morning you'll meet our head gardener, Mr. Hawthorne. If anyone can teach you about this place it's him. His family's been tending these Gardens almost as long as we have."

"A gardener? But I want to stay with my sister," Silas said.

"Our place is outside," Jonquil said. "You'll do more good by working the gardens and learning all you can. Now say goodnight to your sister."

Silas and Lily exchanged goodbyes. As they hugged, she realized that when he was gone she would be alone in this strange house.

"Be careful," she said.

Silas grinned. "I'll be fine. Get some rest." As he

walked out with Jonquil, he turned to his grandmother. "You said the evils here are the ones that escaped when Pandora opened the box. What happened to those still inside? Where is the box?"

"If I knew I would have solved a question that's riddled this house since the moment it came into existence. Prometheus hid it well. Many have spent their lives searching for it, not all for noble purposes. Some wanted to loosen the dark lords that are still harbored within, biding their time to escape."

When they were gone, Deiva went back to the window. "Polly will show you to your room. There is much still to discuss, but I must wait for your grandfather to come home. He should be here any minute."

Lily left her like that, peering out the window through her black veil, waiting for a man decades dead to return.

"Your grandmother is a fine one, a fine one indeed," Polly said as she slid the way up another flight of stairs. "Took me in when no one else would, she did."

They followed a confusing zigzagging path of hallways until they came to a room with a comfortable-looking feather bed and a fireplace that burned merrily. Old photos were displayed on top of a dresser. A stand-up mirror was reversed and facing the wall. Lily's trunk was already there.

"This used to be Miss Abigail's room, it did. That is, until she disappeared all those years ago."

Polly's skin seeped in the light from the fire and her white eyes reflected tiny flames inside of them.

"Who's this?" Lily picked up a photo of two intense looking girls with black hair.

"That's your Grannie Deiva before gilirot got her and that's her little sister Abby. Tragedy it was when that happened." She shook her head. "Pull the bell if you need anything. And words of wisdom to live by: Don't go into any rooms unless you're absolutely certain what they are. This house will play ten tricks to Sunday, it will."

Polly shut the door and left Lily alone for the first time in days. She unpacked her trunk and readied herself for bed. *'Silas and I are trapped,'* she thought and tried to push it away. She took her brush out and began combing her hair, something she always did to calm herself. When she got up to 30 strokes, she turned the mirror around so she could see how she was doing. Lily felt a scream lodge in her throat at the ghastly reflection staring back at her. It was as if she'd been dead for months. Her skin fell away in patches, revealing bones underneath. There were blank holes were her nose should have been. Her hair had fallen out in clumps and, instead of eyes, empty sockets stared back at her. Her arms and legs were rotting flesh covered in a nightgown. She flipped the mirror over and shoved it into the wall so hard she was surprised it didn't break.

Lily climbed into bed and burrowed under the blankets waiting for the nightmare to end.

6

The Green Girl

This wasn't how Silas imagined his first day. His morning started with Arfast booting him out of the pallet in the bunkhouse where he was sleeping.

"Rise and shine, bucko," Arfast said. The three dozen or so dusk riders living in the windowless room with a potbelly stove were drinking coffee from tin cups and struggling into their clothes.

"Listen up," Jonquil told the men. "We've received disturbing reports of mist people turning up dead with no marks of injury on their bodies. I'm taking some riders north to look into what's happening. While I'm gone, Skuld will lead the patrols. I don't need to tell you how dangerous it's been recently or to be careful."

For the rest of the morning, Silas tried to catch his uncle alone, but every time he approached, Jonquil seemed too busy. He finally caught him as his uncle saddled up his horse. The rest of the riders were busy tying down their packs and singing bawdy songs.

"You're to work with Horatio Hawthorne in the Gardens while I'm away" Jonquil said. His face was icy and devoid of emotion. "Listen to him and show you have more brains than your father does. The house is off limits as well."

"But Lily —?"

"— Will do just fine without you under foot. It's time for both of you to grow up. If you ever hope to reach adulthood, you'll heed my words."

Jonquil and the others rode off through a sea of grass into the mist surrounding Nightfall Gardens.

Horatio Hawthorne showed up at the bunkhouse not longer after. He was lean and rangy with a shock of unkempt hair and a walrus mustache. His chin seemed to disappear into his neck. He thrust a hoe into Silas's hands. "Hope you're not afraid of blistering those dainty hands," he said.

They made their way to a vegetable patch first. Silas noticed that the house was ever a presence that loomed over things here. It appeared to have added new balconies and chimneys overnight.

"Oh no, not again," Mr. Hawthorne said, wrenching his hair.

Up ahead, the gate to the garden was smashed to splinters. "Blasted trolls," Mr. Hawthorne said, kicking the trampled carrot garden. "All my hard work, ruined."

Silas studied the remains of the broken fence and earth imprinted with massive footprints. A gray gloom that spelled afternoon thunderstorms hung overhead, though the way the gardener acted, it might as well have been a summer scorcher.

"Can't abide this heat," Mr. Hawthorne said, wiping sweat from his brow. "Riles the trolls something fierce. Well, don't stand there, lad. We have to patch this fence or we'll have every troll in the Gardens sniffing around."

As they worked, Mr. Hawthorne told Silas about his family. "We've tended these gardens, pretty near as long as you Blackwoods have been here. At least that's what my da' used to say. Great-Granddaddy ten times back was an alchemist. He got the call here, like people do. Every time those gates open, somebody wanders in sayin' that they dreamed about the place. Once you get it in your blood, it's hard to leave."

Mr. Hawthorne spit as if the outside world left a bad taste in his mouth. "Don't know how people abide all that sun. Stuffy as the inside of a soggy boot, I say."

Silas, who felt damp and clammy, could have used a little heat. The sky was the color of a dark bruise and the clouds were as gray as day-old mash.

"Anyways, Great-Granddaddy had deep magic and a green thumb. Concocted all manner of potions to make food grow in this blighted place —

and protect the people that live here," Mr. Hawthorne choked up on the last part.

Silas looked up from where he was pounding the last post back in place. Tears were streaming down the gardener's cheeks, leaving tracks on his dirty face.

"Mr. Hawthorne, are you okay?"

"Oh fine, lad. Fine," he said, wiping the tears away with the sleeve of his shirt. "Sometimes old memories bubble up just when you thought you've put them to bed."

The gardener shook the gate to see how sturdy it was. "This won't stop a blind brownie. I need my spell toolbox. Be a good lad and fetch it from my cottage."

"Spell toolbox?"

"Aye, it's full of all kinds of fix-ems. My daughter Cassandra can show you where it is. Just follow this path and whatever you do, don't leave it. No matter what you see or who calls to you. Do you understand?" Mr. Hawthorne clutched him so hard by the wrist that a twinge shot up his arm.

"You're hurting me," Silas said.

"This is nothing compared to what'll happen if you leave the path," Mr. Hawthorne said.

Silas left Mr. Hawthorne and set off down the trail. It was his first time in Nightfall Gardens alone and he tried to map it out in his mind. There seemed to be three distinct gardens that sprawled the length of the house. The furthest was full of dead trees and lush rosebushes that pained his eyes with their color. The next was a maze of hedges so high he couldn't see into it. The one that was closest was the most beautiful. He passed an entrance that sloped toward a massive lawn. Wisteria plants blossomed and scented the air. There were benches for contemplation under shaded cherry trees. At the far end of the lawn was the statue of a hooded figure that was corroded with age. Beyond that, the garden turned to other paths.

"Silas," Lily stepped from behind a tree. She was wearing a red dress that ran to her ankles and her hair was pulled up and tied with red poppies.

"Lily, what are you doing here?" Silas asked. He stopped and took a step toward his sister.

"I wanted to take a walk in the garden. Won't you come with me? It's so lovely in the shade," Lily put out her hand for her brother. Her voice was oddly flat and emotionless.

Silas started for her and remembered what Mr. Hawthorne told him.

"Lily, is there something wrong? Why are you talking that way?"

"Come walk with me where we can always be together," Lily said, in the detached voice. She was standing as close to the path as she could without stepping on it. Her eyes flashed red and blue in the light. As he watched, her shape blurred and solidified.

Silas backed away, his feet crunching upon the gravel of the path. "Lily? Who — who are you?"

"Lily? Who— who are you?" the Lily-double mocked back. The voice was shrill and sounded nothing like his sister now. Her shape blurred again, and this time Silas saw a shadowy figure with claws for hands. When it shifted back to Lily, some pieces of her face weren't where they should have been. One eye was higher than the other. Her jaw sagged.

"Come walk with me. Come walk with me forever," the figure shrieked as Silas fled down the path.

His heart thudded in his chest and his nerves felt as if they were being pulled to the surface of his skin. *'What was that thing?'* he thought. *'How could it look like my sister?'*

Silas followed the path until it led out of the trees and manicured landscape and he came to a cottage and barn in the middle of a field. Behind them sat a hot house through which he could see the outlines of plants growing inside. Not far away, a wall of mist obscured the edge of a forest. He was coming up the walk when he heard beautiful singing from inside the barn.

"Oh, one day, the darkness will go.

Take away all our woes.

Heavy burdens will be put down

And Nightfall Gardens will fall to the ground!"

He came to the entrance of the barn, just as the song ended. Inside, he saw empty horse stalls and a pen holding the fattest cow he'd ever seen. Hay and animal droppings were strewn about the floor.

Pigeons cooed in the rafters overhead.

"Hello?" he said. Silas looked about but saw no one inside.

As if his voice were the cue, a girl jumped out of one of the stalls. He only had time to observe two things before something crashed down on his head, blinding him. She was wielding a pitchfork... and her skin was green.

"Get him! Get him, Osbold," the girl cried. Silas was turned and thrown into a railing. He struck it hard enough to crash through, landing in mud and slop. He reached up, feeling for the bucket that had been dropped on him. Before he could take it off, a foot smashed down on his hand.

"Oh no, you don't," the girl said. "Watch him, Osbold. That's a good boy. Keep your eyes on him."

"Cassandra?" Silas said, hoping he remembered Mr. Hawthorne's daughter's name.

"Don't start your devilry with me, spirit. How did you slip free of the garden?" the girl said, jabbing Silas with the pitchfork. He bit down to keep from screaming.

"I'm Silas Blackwood," he gasped, trying to swallow the pain. "Your father sent me for the spell toolbox."

"Blackwood?" The pressure lessened in his side. "We'll find out about that soon enough."

The bucket was knocked from his head and Silas blinked in the light. Cassandra stood in front of him, pointing the pitchfork at him. Her skin was the green of ivy after a cool rain. Her jasmine eyes narrowed at him. Even her blond hair was tinged the color of a fresh sprig.

"Watch him, Osbold," she said. Something grunted at his side. Silas saw leathery wings, a dog-like face and curved horns. The creature couldn't have been more than two feet tall. It thrust its chest forward and gave a pitifully thin squawk.

"What — what is it?" Silas said. He propped himself up on his elbows in the mud.

"Are you daft?" Cassandra said. She plucked a vial from a wooden toolbox and tossed it to him. "It's a gargoyle... runt of the litter. Mother and father didn't want him. Now drink that and we'll find out what your true shape is."

"Drink it?" Silas eyed the milky concoction in the vial skeptically.

"That is, if you don't want to meet the end of my pitchfork again. I don't care who your family is."

Silas unstopped the bottle, smelled the putrid substance inside, and swallowed it as quickly as he could. The liquid burned going down. His stomach churned as though he was going to throw it up but somehow he didn't. After a minute, Cassandra pulled the pitchfork back and stood it against the barn wall. "See, now that wasn't so hard. Was it?" Osbold flew across the room and landed on her shoulder.

Silas climbed to his feet and felt his sore side. "Do you always greet guests like that?"

"We don't get too many people making house

calls here," she said. "Usually, it's Shades or other nasties that have managed to free themselves from their garden. Didn't used to happen so much, but these days nothing is to be trusted."

Cassandra lobbed him another bottle. "Put this where the pitchfork kissed you and you'll be healed in no time."

Silas scooped some of the greasy ointment from the bottle and rubbed it on his chest. He immediately felt a cooling sensation. "Thanks," he said.

Cassandra picked up the toolbox and handed it to him. They came close to touching in the exchange and she jerked away, making Silas lose his grip. The toolbox fell and something glass broke inside.

"Clumsy oaf," she said angrily. Cassandra knelt and opened the box. Inside, a vial full of purple liquid was shattered and turning to smoke. "Tracker spray. It helps you find the way if you're lost. Luckily, it wasn't something worse." She stood up and looked down at him. "Next time, be more careful."

"You're the one that made me drop it," Silas said. He was hard to anger, but once he started there was no turning back. He reached to snatch the toolbox from Cassandra and again, she jumped away from him. This time, he gripped the handle and didn't drop it. "Afraid, I'll bite?" he said.

Osbold growled in his throat and his wings fanned out. Cassandra pouted as though she'd bit into a sour apple. "You Blackwoods are insufferable."

Silas stomped off without a further word. When he passed the garden where he'd seen the fake Lily, there was nothing but empty lawn and the statue of the hooded figure. Mr. Hawthorne was on his knees examining the damaged crop when he returned. "Not nearly as bad as I thought," he said. "We'll put so many spells on the fence they won't know Fee-Fi-Fo-Fum from Fiddle-De-Dee."

Mr. Hawthorne opened the spell toolbox and rummaged through vials and bottles of all shapes and sizes. "Essence of owls' bane, goblin sweat, mermaid tears, now where is it? Ah hah!" He found what he was looking for and circled the fence, sprinkling the clear liquid on the wood while muttering an incantation.

"See anything unusual along the way?" the gardener asked as he finished with the first bottle. He took another out and started pacing the fence again.

"I saw something that looked like my sister, only it wasn't," Silas said. He followed the gardener, lugging the toolbox. "What was it?"

"A Shade, most likely," Mr. Hawthorne said. "That's the White Garden, where all of death's surrogates live. Being dead, they despise the living. Demons, Banshees, Succubi, the Lords of the Underworld, the Wicked Crones —all call it home. Death itself is nothing to be afeard of, of course, but these are the creatures that suck the marrow from the living and rob them of life's natural end. They'll try to seduce you, but as long as you don't leave the path, they can do no harm."

"Cassandra said they sometimes get out of the garden," Silas said.

Mr. Hawthorne wiped his neck. "This wretched heat is too much. Aye, she's right. But not just there; evils are breaking out from all the gardens."

"Why?"

"Waiting for your Gran to pass, more than likely. Happens whenever a new Blackwood takes over. Least that's what I'm told. I've only known Deiva. Think this should about do it." The gardener put his hands on his hips and eyed their handiwork.

They spent the rest of the day planting pink and yellow vespertines in front of the mansion. Silas kept careful watch of the windows but never caught a glimpse of his sister.

"Twilight-blooming flowers repel spirits trying to find a way inside. This old house has more than enough creepy crawlies already," Mr. Hawthorne said. "I don't understand how Deiva and the others stand it, cooped up there all day."

Gloomy gray dusk was turning to night. The gardener leaned against his shovel. Wolves howled off in the mist.

"Well, we'd better get along, lad. It's none too safe after the red moon rises," he said. They followed another path to the bunkhouse and passed near a stone circle with a sundial in its middle.

"At first light, I'll give you a tour of the gardens and then we'll start digging an irrigation ditch for the new field I want to plant. Too much work and never enough time," Mr. Hawthorne said.

The dusk riders were sharing wine out of skins and playing jimmy knife when Silas came in, not long afterward.

"Couldn't hit the side of a hellcat," one of the riders, flush with drink, yelled. He was stout, with three day's growth on his cheeks. The other riders laughed.

Arfast was 20 paces from a beam gouged with nicks from all the knives that had struck there before. A crude circle was drawn on the beam and two knives barely larger than a letter opener were stuck deep in the wood. He whipped a handful of knives out of his wolf's cloak and began juggling them.

"I wouldn't be so sure about that, Larkspur," Arfast said. "Of course, if you're certain we *could* make a friendly wager."

"Wager? And what would that be?" Larkspur said. He sat forward and slapped his knee with laughter. The other dusk riders roared along with him. "The jimmy knives are too thin and weigh too little. They won't carry that far."

"What if I prove you wrong?" Arfast said.

"I'll skinny dip in Leech Lake," Larkspur said. He took a long pull on his wine skin and it dribbled down his cheeks.

"Not good enough," Arfast said. "I want some of that tobacco you brought back when the gates were open."

Larkspur scratched his chin. "How much?"

"Five smokes."

"It can't be done," the mountainous rider said. "You're mad."

"And I'm telling you, I can get *these* knives in that circle," Arfast said.

"For argument's sake, let's say I win. What do I get?"

"What do you want?" Arfast asked.

"I like that dappled gray that you ride," Larkspur said. He winked at the other dusk riders and they laughed. "It'd handle my considerable bulk well."

"All right, then," Arfast said. "Do we have ourselves a deal?"

"Who am I to turn down such a sweet offering? Deal," Larkspur said. He spit on his palm and shook with Arfast to seal the pact.

Silas looked around at the room. There were a dozen or more riders crowded inside. With the exception of Larkspur, they were a hard, grizzled-looking bunch. Arfast was the youngest, except for himself. Skuld sat at a table alone. His cloak was thrown open to expose the tapered nub of his right arm. Some riders played cards at another table. A bluish haze from the oil lamps filled the air. Everyone watched as Arfast took the knives and readied to throw them.

"Okay. I'm going to put these knives in that post, all the way from here," Arfast said.

"In a blind pig's eye," Larkspur said.

"The last time I checked, your eyesight was perfect," Arfast said. The riders ached with laughter and even Skuld smiled.

Larkspur's lips tightened. "Do it and stop your babbling."

"All right, then," Arfast said. He turned toward Silas who was standing at the entry. "Come here, boy."

"Me?" Silas said. He took a step back as all eyes turned towards him.

"Do you see any other boys here?" Arfast said.

Silas approached as though weights were tied to his feet.

"Yes?"

Arfast bent and grinned at him. "Be a good lad and go put my jimmy knives in that bull's-eye for me."

"What foolery is this? Larkspur roared. He stood up so quickly that his chair fell over. His massive gut quivered with rage.

Arfast handed the knives to Silas and pointed him towards the bulls-eye. "I didn't say *how* I would get the knives there."

"Cheating little —," Larkspur lunged for Arfast as the room erupted with laughter and cheers. Two of the riders grabbed him by the arms and pulled him back. Silas walked down the aisle and shoved the knives into the center of the target.

After his initial anger wore off, Larkspur chuckled at how he'd been outwitted. "I'll be more careful with my words the next time," he said, handing over the tobacco he'd rolled. Arfast put an arm around the big man. "If it's any consolation, I don't think I'll be able to pull that trick again."

The lamps were turned down as the riders retreated to their bunks. Soon the night gave way to the sounds of snoring and men breathing heavily. The night shift headed out for patrol. Silas was preparing for bed when a hand fell on his shoulder. Skuld could only be half-seen in the light.

"How was your first day?" he asked.

Silas told him about the vegetable patch and plantings they had done.

"Then you had a more useful day than us. Devilish quiet out there. I don't like it," he said.

"When will Jonquil be back?"

"Could be a week, could be next month. Depends how deep in the fog he has to go. Now get some sleep, lad."

It wasn't long before the lamps were extinguished and Silas was fast asleep. He dreamed intensely but remembered nothing. When he came to, it was the middle of the night and he saw a crack of moonlight as the bunkhouse door closed.

'Who's up at this time?' he thought. Silas slid from his mat and crept to the door. The other riders were sleeping. One of them muttered in his slumber. *'Something doesn't feel right,'* Silas thought. He pushed open the well-oiled door and slipped

into night. Clouds swept across the sky, obscuring the hanging fruit moon. Insects sang from nearby fields. For a moment, he thought he had lost the person who snuck from the cabin, but then he saw a form striding toward the mist, his wolf head cloak pulled up so he couldn't tell which rider it was.

Silas dropped off the porch and followed the figure. The dew was heavy on the ground and soon his pants legs were soaked. Little patches of mist curled in the air as he neared the trees. The fog became heavier as he entered the forest and it wasn't long before he could see no further than a few feet in front of him.

He thought he'd lost the rider completely when suddenly he came into a clearing. The mist was so thick Silas almost stepped into the rider before spotting him. The man was turned away facing the woods. Silas crouched behind a tree. The wait didn't last long. Something stirred in the trees. A wolf with a tattered white coat loped from the forest. One side of his face had been mauled when he was younger for no fur grew there. The skin was puckered and scarred.

"Did you get what I requested?" the wolf growled.

"I did, sire," the rider said, bowing to his knees.

"And it's true that the girl is here?" the wolf continued.

"Yes, my lord," the man said.

Heavy tendrils of fog covered them for a

moment. It was so thick, Silas thought, that if he touched it, the mist might be solid. Wolves howled from every direction. A breeze parted the mist and they were visible again.

"Good, then our time is almost come. Soon, the Gardens will be ours and all the foul things inside will spill forth to reclaim the world."

The wind grew stronger and it ruffled Silas's shirt collar and cooled his neck. He tried to submerge the terror he felt. The wolf with the ravaged face sniffed the air.

"You were followed," he snarled.

"It can't be. I put a dream draught in the other riders' wine. They won't wake until morning," the man said.

"Fool!" The wolf said. He took a menacing step toward the rider.

"I'm sorry, my liege," the rider said and fell to his knees.

Silas backed away, trying to keep his legs from collapsing with fear. He found the trail and ran through the mist toward the bunkhouse. Trees appeared and disappeared around him. The darkness felt like a living presence. A stitch burned in his side as he burst into the open. The bunkhouse was ahead and Nightfall Gardens towered over everything as usual. A solitary light burned in one of its windows. Silas looked over his shoulder and a scream ripped from his throat. The wolf was bearing down on him. His mangled face was pulled back revealing fangs the size of paring knives. For every step Silas took, the wolf gained three.

"Help!" Silas yelled. "Somebody help me!" Nobody answered. For one moment, he thought he heard laughter coming from the Gardens but the next it sounded like the tall grass swishing around him. The wolf was almost on him. *'Turn and fight,'* he thought. It was his only option. True, he'd be ripped limb from limb but at least he'd be facing the enemy. *'I'm sorry, Lily,'* he thought. Silas spun.

The wolf was seconds away. His eyes blazed with fury. The wolf landed in front of Silas and growled. "It's been a long time since I've killed a Blackwood. This will be a treat."

Silas couldn't have imagined what would have happened if a lone figure on a white horse hadn't raced from the mist at that moment. The man was gaunt, with receding white hair and pale blue eyes. He was dressed in a white cloak with light chain mail, and he hoisted a sword above him. The ground shook as he vaulted the distance between Silas and the wolf.

"Not you," the wolf said. "Not now."

The rider said nothing. He only cantered his horse and blocked the way to Silas.

"Thank you," Silas said. The man looked down at him and nodded. There was something oddly familiar about his face. The red moon broke through the clouds and for one second, Silas could see through the man. He was insubstantial, a ghost. He gestured for the boy to go.

Silas turned and ran. He was almost back to the bunkhouse before it occurred to him why the man looked so familiar. *'That ghost was my grandfather,'* he thought.

7

Locked in Nightfall Manor

Lily was left to explore the house every day, except for in the afternoons, when Polly brought her to Deiva's room. Her grandmother never seemed to leave her chair near the window. "I want to make sure that I see him when he comes back," she told Lily.

Once, Lily did see her grandfather. Deiva was telling her the history of the mist people. "They're descended from a band of gypsies that entered when the gates were open and asked to play music for our family. When they realized what this place was, they never wanted to leave. We told them they could have the land that leads into the mist. No one knows how far or deep it goes. You lose the ability to see after a while." Deiva was this far into the story when she cried out and pointed out the window. "There he is. Do you see him? He's come home!" Lily looked out the window and saw a man with long white hair canter out of the fog on a horse. He stopped and stared at the house as though looking straight at them. Then, he disappeared back into the mist. "No!" Deiva shouted. "Not again. Not for the thousandth time." Minutes later, her grandmother was complaining about the rain and seemed to have forgotten she'd just seen the ghost of her husband. "I do hope he comes home soon," She said. "No one catches cold more quickly than him."

Lily soon realized that it would never be truly possible to know the house. There were knowable things and then there was the unknowable that surrounded her at all times and filled her with a sense of dread. On the knowable front were the employees that made the great house hum. Ozy, the butler, was a mummified old man whose main duty consisted of making sure the dinner table was set. The dining room was a luxurious affair as big as a train depot with intricate molding on the ceiling and ornate paintings on the walls. Since Deiva refused to leave her bedroom, Lily ate there alone. Ozy shuffled about, his skin so dry it fell off him like snowflakes as he served the dishes. He had a hooked nose and the fire of life sparked dim in his eyes. Under his faded suit, Lily saw gray bandages wrapped around most of his body. He rarely said a word, except for "Anything else, my lady?"

Ursula cleaned Lily's room every morning. Her

face was elfin and her arms were covered in thick spidery hair. A unibrow formed a solid line over her large eyes. Lily had never met such a happy person in her life. "Beautiful day, miss. Nothing like a great big rain cloud blowing in to cheer one up," she'd say with a smile, or, "You're looking a little green under the gills today, Miss. Wonderful, Wonderful." Not matter how cheery her disposition, Lily felt depressed when the chambermaid was around. Sometimes a black haze descended over her and she would lie in bed, crying and feeling hopeless as the young girl whistled a funeral dirge and swept her room. "There, there, Miss. You've got to stay upbeat. Just remember it'll get worse before it gets better." As soon as Ursula finished cleaning and left the room, Lily's mood would immediately lighten. It was Polly who told her why that was. "She's a Glumpog, poor thing," the housemaid said. "Nicest girl you'd ever meet, but the death of the party. Her kind feeds off sadness and depression. It fills the room wherever they are and she can't do anything about it, the dear." After that, Lily made sure to be gone before Ursula stopped by for her morning cleaning.

There were other staff Lily saw flitting down the halls toward their appointed task, but those two and the housemaid were the most consistent presences in her life over the next couple of weeks. Polly was the one who exerted the greatest influence over the house and was also the one that stopped her when Lily tried sneaking out through one of the many entrances. "Now where exactly do you think you're going, miss?" The housemaid slithered in front of her as Lily prepared to go out a glass door into one of the gardens. "I need fresh air," Lily said, annoyed. "The air out there might kill you, miss," Polly replied, leaving slug tracks as she closed the door. She smiled, and Lily saw that the maid didn't have teeth, only white gums. "No, much safer in here, where you can be protected." Another time, Lily decided to sneak out in the middle of the night, but when she opened her bedroom door, she saw a white cocoon as big as a person was hanging from the ceiling. She stared at the dripping mess and then the shell broke open. Polly's face, wet and gleaming, shoved through the side. "It's not safe to roam these halls at night, ma'am," she said. Lily was so stunned that she turned back without a word and went to bed.

When she wasn't trying to escape, Lily spent her time exploring the vast, drafty house that changed its shape depending on the day. Sometimes the house would have four floors, sometimes five and other times seven. Rooms would move and one evening she wandered for hours searching for her bedroom. One afternoon, Lily packed a lunch, determined to walk the whole house, but didn't finish a floor before it was too dark to see. "Nightfall Gardens lets you know what it wants you to," Polly said when Lily dragged herself back exhausted. There were ground rules the maid laid down before she allowed Lily to go on her jaunts. "Never enter a room with closed doors, no matter who or what you hear inside. When you come to the old part of the house where the walls turn to stone, don't go further. Never go into the attic. That's something you could ask Mr. Thomas and Mrs. Moira if they were about."

Lily went a week before breaking the first rule. She was on the third floor, looking for a room with an open door, she'd discovered the day before. The room had two armoires filled with women's dresses that looked as though they might have been in style a century before. The dresses were long and colorful with big hoops under the skirts. There was a chest stuffed with wide-brimmed hats with ostrich feathers. She'd spent the day trying on dresses and imagining walking the streets of Paris.

She was beginning to give up hope she'd ever find the room again when her mother called from behind a closed door. "Lily, Lily, help! Your father and I are locked up here." If she'd thought about it, she would never have opened the door; after all, her mother was on the other side of the gates, and if it was her, how could she know it was Lily that was passing? But the voice was so undoubtedly Moira's that Lily threw the door open without a second thought.

Light, gray and overcast, filtered through a window into the bedroom. It must have belonged to a girl at one time. A canopy with white netting hid the figures lying on the bed. The wallpaper was pink and patterned with tridents and sea monsters. A gold music box was open on a dresser. One wall of the room was stacked high with porcelain dolls, glass-eyed, with fake hair. Their faces were painted with red lipstick and each wore clothing from a different period in time. She saw lords, ladies, footman, clowns, sailors, babies, and more. If she'd been in New Amsterdam, Lily would have stopped and admired them in a storefront, thinking of all the things she'd buy when she was the toast of the city, but now they barely registered.

"Mother," Lily said, "is that you?" She crept across the room to the bed. Two figures were shadowed behind the curtain.

"Hurry, before they come back. Untie us," Moira said.

Lily saw her mother thrashing on the bed, trying to break free. "Hang on and I'll —." She yanked the netting away and stumbled back in terror. Two life-sized dolls were laid across the bed. Their glass eyes shifted towards her. Their fake eyelashes blinked. The dolls were porcelain copies of her mother and father.

"Come give your mother a hug," the Moira doll said, pulling itself up from the bed.

Lily scrambled backward towards the open door. She saw movement around her. The dolls were coming to life. The Moira and Thomas dolls stood and jerked toward her as if being pulled by invisible strings. Sharp pain shot through her ankle, and Lily lost her balance and fell to the floor.

A red tin soldier with a rifle and a needle-sized bayonet was stabbing her over and over in the ankle. Lily kicked and sent the toy flying across the room. Something grabbed her hair and started pulling. Lily reached back, grabbing the doll and flinging it into a wall. She pulled herself to her feet as more dolls reached for her. Lily took two springing steps away from them on her good ankle and grabbed the wall for support. The dolls were swarming her, yanking her dress, trying to pull her down. The door was maddeningly close. Ceramic hands encircled her throat and she was staring into the shifting glass eyes of the Moira doll. Lily felt the air being crushed from her. Her dress ripped as the smaller dolls tried to topple her. Lily's vision clouded as the last of the air was choked out of her. *'So nice to rest,'* she thought. A vision of her family weeping and standing around her grave came to her then, and she kicked at the dolls that clung to her legs. Her hand searched a nearby table. It found nothing but empty space, until at last her fingers touched a candelabra. She swung it into the face of the Moira doll with the last of her strength. The doll's face exploded into tiny shards and the hands loosened their grip. She struck it again and again, smashing it to dust. The Thomas doll reached for her and Lily turned on him, shattering his head with a blow. He fell lifeless to the floor. As she watched, the other dolls fled underneath the bed and into a closet. Lily hopped outside of the room and shut the door, dropping the candelabra on the carpet. She leaned against the wall and felt hot tears in her eyes. For one moment she'd actually believed it was her parents, and now they'd been taken away from her again.

Lily didn't tell anyone about what had happened in the room and no one asked, not even Polly, when she limped in to see her grandmother the next afternoon. If the maid had eyebrows she might have raised them, but instead she looked straight at Lily and left her and Deiva without a word.

One of her favorite rooms in the house was a sitting room that overlooked the Shadow Garden. The room had three large windows that ran from the floor to the ceiling, comfortable chairs for afternoon tea, and a fireplace that was scrolled with ironwork. From here, Lily could see all the way out to the mist behind the gardens. She looked for Silas through a brass telescope that Ursula brought her but never saw him or Jonquil, though once she did see Skuld leading horsemen along a path as though they were searching for something.

The Shadow Garden was aptly named. It always seemed to be dark over the trees and winding paths, as though what dusky light fell on the rest of Nightfall Gardens was unable to penetrate that area. The trees were twisted and stunted; many of them were dead. Rosebushes bloomed so bright that they could almost blind a person. Lily sometimes saw shapes moving through its grounds, but when she focused the telescope there was nothing there.

One stormy day, when the wind was so strong that the rain blew sideways and the house shook, Lily saw three women walking along one of the paths in the garden. The women wore white gowns and had the palest skin Lily had ever seen in her life. They put their hands out to feel the rain. Ursula entered with a pot of steaming tea on a tray and, as always happened when the maid was near, Lily's mood turned hopeless and forlorn. "Who are those women?" She asked. "Wot women, me lady?" Ursula replied. "The three walking in the Shadow Garden," Lily said. *'Though, I don't know why it should matter,'* she thought. *'Life is terribly pointless. The most a person can hope for is a tombstone that's spelled correctly when they die.'* Lily shook her head to push the dark thoughts away. The teapot and cups clattered on the tray. Ursula's nose twitched and her chin quivered. Her unibrow furrowed. "Is something wrong?" Lily asked. "Beggin' your pardon, tho — those are the Smiling Ladies," Ursula said. She dropped the tray on a table and leaned against a chair for support. *'She's scared witless,'* Lily thought. "And who are they?" she asked. "Someone you don't want to meet, unless you're ready for eternal sleep. Excuse me, I've said too much," Ursula said, fleeing the room. As soon as she was gone, Lily's mood lightened. She looked back through the telescope, but the women were gone.

When she'd been at Nightfall Gardens for more

than a month and was going crazy from loneliness and boredom, Lily finally made a friend. She was in the sitting room, scanning the Shadow Garden, when Polly glided in, followed by a girl who was near her age. The girl was taller than she was and wore a brown woolen dress. Her hair was blond, tinged with the same color green as her skin. The girl shifted uncomfortably and scowled at her.

"You're green," Lily said stunned.

"Observant as her brother," Cassandra said to Polly. "These Blackwoods are sharp ones."

Polly slid across the floor, leaving a slimy track in her wake. She put a sticky hand on Lily's shoulder. "You'll have to excuse me, my lady," the maid said.

"What for?"

"It's been a long time since we've had a child in the house, and those that live here are used to our solitary ways. We forget what it's like to feel alone. I thought you might like to meet the only girl your age in the gardens."

"Who is she?"

"Cassandra, the groundskeeper's daughter."

"And why is her skin green?"

"That's a question best saved for her," Polly whispered. "Though truth be told, I'd wait until I knew her better. She has a bit of a temper."

The maid oozed out of the room and left the girls alone. They stared at each other in silence until Cassandra spoke. "So how long is this going to take?" she asked.

"Is what going to take?" Lily replied, curious about the new girl.

"Being here, in the house. I have lots of work and none of it's going to get done while I'm inside. Not all of us are allowed the luxury of a cup of a hot tea on a chilly afternoon," Cassandra said, irritated.

"You think I *want* to be here?" Lily snapped. "That I wouldn't rather be back in New Amsterdam or anywhere but this drafty house where every room is haunted and I can't see my brother or parents?"

"You're a Blackwood. This is where you belong, your royal highness," Cassandra said, mocking her with a curtsy. "Now, if you'll excuse me —." She backed towards the door.

"You said you knew my brother," Lily interjected. In the city, she would never have talked with the children of the people who worked backstage at the theaters where they played. Silas was the kind-hearted one, the one who stopped to comfort the stagehand's daughter when she skinned her knee or who made fast friends with the street urchins that lived nearby. Even then, Lily had dreamed of bigger things, grand parties and newspaper headlines proclaiming her the toast of Europe. One month at Nightfall Gardens, unable to confide in anyone, had broken her down. She was desperate for contact with anyone, including this green-skinned girl.

"Oh, I know him. Stuck a pitchfork in his side

because I thought he was a Shade," Cassandra said. She itched at the dress as though she wasn't used to wearing such finery.

Lily came out of the chair. "What? Is he all right?"

"Hardheaded as ever," Cassandra said. Her expression loosened when she saw how concerned Lily was. "Gave him a healing potion. He was back to being a nuisance in no time. Shouldn't have snuck up on Osbold and me."

"Who's Osbold?" Lily asked.

"My gargoyle," Cassandra said.

"You have a gargoyle?" Lily said in wonder.

"Is everything a question with you? Of course I do. They won't allow him in here though. Technically he's a creature of the Gardens. Not that the slug of a housekeeper and other staff aren't," Cassandra came to the window and peered at the Shadow Garden. "Never been in the house before," she said, rubbing her hand against the chair. "Not much call for the gardener's daughter to come calling."

"Let me show you around. At least what I know of it," Lily said. She reached for Cassandra, but the gardener's daughter jerked away as if scalding water had been thrown on her. "You mustn't ever – no one can touch me!" She backed into the curtains.

"What's wrong? I didn't mean any harm," Lily said.

"Neither do I, but harm is what will happen if you or anyone touches my skin," she said.

"What do you mean?"

"Beggin' your pardon, ma'am, may I be excused?" Cassandra asked. The toughness was back in her eyes.

"Not until we get some custard puffs from the kitchen," Lily said, wanting more conversation from the green girl, even if it meant taking her abuse for a while longer.

The kitchen was on the ground floor in the back of house. Lily filled a plate with the puffs and they sat and ate them on the main stairwell. While they were eating, a door slammed upstairs and they heard horrible moaning, followed by running feet thudding down the hallway. Polly came into the entry, a moment later with a broom in her hand. "Who knows what kind of ugly has broke free this time," she said, gliding past them and up the stairs.

"Does this happen all the time?" Cassandra asked.

"They say it didn't used to be so bad," Lily said, setting the empty plate on the stairs.

"But your gran is dying," Cassandra said.

"Yes," Lily said bitterly. "And when she does I'm expected to take over and spend my life here."

"It's the lot of the Blackwoods," Cassandra said.

"But I didn't do anything." Lily balled her hands into fists.

"Doesn't matter. We all bear the burden of those who went before us," Cassandra said.

"What do you know?" Lily asked exasperated.

"A sight more than a city girl from outside the

gates. I've grown up with a fear that at any moment something could happen and I'd die. Stray an inch off of the paths and something will grab you. Wake up in the night with a tree branch scratching at your window and every nightmare you've ever had is outside your door."

"How — how do you stand it?" Lily asked.

"It's what I know," Cassandra said. "How long do you think I would fit in out there —," she gestured toward the nothingness beyond the wall that separated the house from the world. "— looking like I do." She stood to leave. "On that note, I have to go. Osbold is going crazy without me and I need to help my father finish the planting."

Cassandra was at the door when Lily called out. "Can you come back again?"

The green girl stopped in the open door. "Why?"

"Because I don't have any friends and I need someone to help me explore the house."

Cassandra gave her a hard look and then made up her mind. "Okay, friends it is. I'll come again in two days."

"One more thing, please."

"What?"

"Tell my brother to take care of himself and that I love him," Lily said.

Cassandra chewed her lips. "I try to avoid him when possible. But I'll pass along what you said."

That night, Deiva seemed in a better mood than

usual. One of the windows was cracked to let out the sour stench of the gilirot that was eating her alive. She wore her usual black dress with a veil covering her face, but it was pressed and washed. Candles illuminated every corner of the room. She was even drinking a glass of red wine, raising the veil to take dainty sips, accidentally giving Lily glimpses of the weeping sores that covered her face.

"There she is, my beautiful granddaughter and my ticket away from here someday — but not tonight, mind you. Tonight, we drink and celebrate," she said.

"What are we celebrating?" Lily asked, taking the glass her grandmother thrust into her hand.

"Abigail, my dear, we're celebrating my sister Abigail," Deiva said. She gently tweaked Lily on the nose and fell back into her chair.

"What's the occasion?" Lily said, taking a seat across from her grandmother. The red moon was up and looked large enough to swallow the house, gardens and all.

"It's her birthday, my dear. She disappeared many, many years ago. How is it possible you know none of this? Your father will get a scolding, the next time I see him. He kept you in secrecy about your birthright."

'*And bless him for that,*' Lily thought. How horrible it would have been to know what her destiny was.

"My sister, for all of her virtues, was unable to

accept her lot in life," Deiva continued. "She was obsessed with finding a way of freeing us from Nightfall Gardens and trapping the things that live here so they could never get out."

Lily's heart raced in her chest. "Is such a thing possible?"

"Of course not. Don't you think we would have found it if there was?" Deiva said. "It's a family legend. Nothing more. Believe me, plenty of Blackwoods have gone mad trying to find a way to free us of this curse. Abigail paid for it with her life."

"How do you know that?" Lily asked. If there was a way to close Nightfall Gardens and make sure nothing ever escaped, then she could have a career on the stage.

"Because she told me," Deiva said. "Not two hours ago when she came to visit. Of course she came tonight. It's her birthday."

Candle light illuminated Deiva as she raised her veil to take a drink of wine. Lily stared into a far corner so she wouldn't see the disease that was rotting her grandmother. Deiva caught her looking away and laughed. "Does my appearance disgust you? There was a time when I was a vain little peacock like you, but your grandfather's absence stripped me of that. Then the gili got hold of me and took the last of my illusions."

"What — what happened to Abigail?" Lily asked. She waited until the veil fluttered back over Deiva's chin before she looked in her direction.

"How did she disappear?"

"How does anyone? One moment she was here and the next she was gone. She was acting strange months before she ever vanished. Abby spent all of her time in our ancestral library, reading the history of our family and scouring the ancient tomes that are there."

"We have a family library?" Lily asked.

"Oh my dear, I forget how little you know. Yes, we do. That is, if you can find it. The room moves around, like many in Nightfall Gardens do."

Something screamed, deep and terrible, outside in the dark, as though it was being killed, and Lily jumped in her seat. Deiva looked out the window at the twisted trees and mysterious vegetation that led into a wall of fog.

"The gardens are restless, much like they were on the night Abby disappeared. The dusk riders were busy with all the breaks that had happened and evils that were loosed. Several of the riders died. No one knew my sister was gone until the next morning."

Deiva was the one to discover Abigail's empty chamber, the one Lily was living in now. Her bed hadn't been slept in and there was no evidence that she tried to sneak out of the house or that one of the spirits of the gardens might have gotten her.

"The gate was closed, so she couldn't have gotten out that way, either," Deiva said. "The only thing we ever found was a sapphire pendent of hers that one of the maids discovered in a hallway on the fifth floor."

"What do you think happened?" Lily asked.

"This house — this house is almost as dangerous as out there," her grandmother said, gesturing outside the window. "Abby poked and prodded until the house took her. She told me that she was close to finding out a way to end the curse. But I didn't believe her. I still don't." Deiva's head lowered on her chin. She was growing tired from the wine.

"When your sister visited tonight, what did she say?" Lily asked.

"Hmmm," Deiva shook her head to rid herself of slumber. "She said to give you a message — to be careful — that you're the last of the Blackwood women and great evils are coming for you. I could have told you that and saved her the trouble. The beings in the Gardens have been trying to kill us as long as this place has existed."

Her grandmother nodded off shortly after that. Lily watched Deiva's veil flutter in and out with sleep and quietly slipped from the room. Noises came from several of the doors on the way back to her room. Icy voices cajoling her to come inside, things that thumped and rolled on the floors. Hysterical tittering came from behind one door and ocean waves crashing against a beach came from another. Lily tuned them out as she had ever since the incident with the dolls.

She was thinking over her great-aunt's disappearance when she turned down the hall toward her bedroom and saw the girl coming out of her room. The girl was near her age, with straight black hair and a pinched face.

"Hey, what are you doing?" Lily said surprised.

The girl looked directly at her and then turned and fled down the hall in the opposite direction.

"Wait! Who are you?" Lily yelled, though the face looked oddly familiar. It was one she'd seen before.

The girl didn't respond, just kept running. *'Oh no you don't,'* Lily thought, taking off after her. It would have been wiser to wake Polly and tell her what happened, but by that time the girl would have gotten away. Also, Lily never again wanted to see the cocoon the housekeeper slept inside.

She chased the girl to the end of the hall and up a narrow flight of stairs to the fourth and fifth floor. On the fifth floor only a few gas lamps sputtered along the halls, making it difficult to see. The hall was dark and quiet. Its walls were covered in ornate gold wallpaper peeling away to reveal the exposed wood underneath.

Lily saw the girl running in and out of shadows, her long, old-fashioned dress held up so she could go faster. "Hey wait, stop!" Lily shouted, but the girl didn't stop. Behind Lily, the gas lamps began extinguishing, one by one, leaving only impenetrable darkness and the light that was ahead of her. Near the end of the hall, the girl, stopped and looked back at Lily. They stared at each other long enough for Lily to realize who it was, and then the girl opened a door and went into a room. "Abigail!" Lily said, but it was too late. The girl was on the other side of the door. Lily's heart beat frantically in her chest. Why had her great-aunt lead her to this room? At the other end of the hall, the lamps began to go dark with a hiss. Soon, the hallway would be black as a tomb and she would be trapped. The second-to-last lamp went out and now the only light left came from a lamp across the hall. Lily remembered Polly's instructions never to enter a room with a closed door. As the last gas lamp went dark, Lily turned the knob and entered the room.

8

Whispers of Eldritch

"Come on, lad. Put your back into it," Mr. Hawthorne said. The groundskeeper was fanning himself with a hat as though it were the middle of summer and not another dusk-gray day where rain looked like it would fall at any time.

Silas was finishing planting the last row of witch vine on the south side of Nightfall Gardens. One thing he'd learned in the last six weeks was that the house needed constant fortification against the forces of darkness. Whether it was dragon's heart by the doors, tiger's jaw under the windows or any of the hundred other species that protected the house, he and Mr. Hawthorne spent a good part of each day, making sure everything was blooming. Withered plants were removed and fresh ones planted. Every week, a section of the house was uprooted and replanted. "Sometimes a plant can look perfectly healthy but all its magic is gone," Mr. Hawthorne told him. "The house is under constant assault from the things wot live here. Nothing they'd love better than to get at your sister."

Silas finished planting the last witch vine and wiped sweat from his forehead. His skin was beaded with dirt and sweat and he daydreamed about a hot bath instead of the cold buckets of water he poured over himself at the end of each workday. He was leaner than when he'd arrived and his hair curled to his eyebrows. He leaned against the hoe and looked up at the windows, but as usual there was no sign of Lily.

"Let's go, lad. This wheelbarrow isn't going to fill itself, and soon dark will come. Best be away from the Gardens when that happens," Mr. Hawthorne said. Thirty minutes later, they set off past the Shadow Garden. By now, Silas knew all three of the gardens, at least in theory. Mr. Hawthorne had given him a guided tour his second day and told him not to mind anything he might see. "Most of the beasties don't know where they are anymore, but the ones that do will do anything to make you stray from the path. Remember, you're safe as long as you don't leave the trail. Once you're in the Garden proper, heaven have mercy on you."

The Shadow Garden was the most foul of all of them for it was the one that was conjured by the human mind. Rosebushes bloomed so vibrantly that it was as though they were fed on blood. White trees leeched of their color stretched into the depths of the property. No insects sang there and a chill came from within, like cold off an ice block. Light seemed to evaporate when it hit the edge of the dark grass. Inside the Shadow Garden, there were plenty of spaces to hide and watch. "Three gardens for the three evils that gorged on human misery," Mr. Hawthorne recited as though it were something he'd learned as a child. "The Labyrinth for the old gods, the Shadow Gardens for the monsters sprung from the imagination, and the White Garden for the spirits that make a mockery of death."

Silas pushed the wheelbarrow ahead of him along the smooth path. The red moon that was always a ghost on the horizon was beginning to creep up in the gray sky. Mr. Hawthorne was following him, lecturing about plants as he did every evening on their way home, when something stirred in the trees beside them. Silas thought he saw movement out of the corner of his eye, but when he looked, he only saw bleached trees shaking with the evening breeze. "Highly lethal to humans if eaten, but one of the most powerful magics if used properly," Mr. Hawthorne said, explaining the different beneficial properties of Blood Creeper extract. Silas thought that if the groundskeeper were cleaned up, his thick mustache trimmed and he were given a tweed jacket, he would look like one of the college professors the Blackwood family played for in Waxahachie. He glanced back, feeling a burst of warmth for his mentor, and that was when he saw the woman watching from the trees. She was beautiful, but not in the same way as his sister or mother. They were universal beauties who could turn the heads of royalty or beggars on the streets; this woman's beauty resided in her earthiness and the smile that lingered about her red lips, even though she was long dead.

"Horatio," the woman said. Her voice was barely above a whisper and sounded of the night.

"Faster, lad," Mr. Hawthorne said ignoring her. Silas could see fear and something else in the groundskeeper's eyes.

"Are you afraid to stop and talk with your wife?" the woman asked. Her voice seemed to come from all around them. She was standing apart from the trees now, and in the red moonlight he saw how much Cassandra resembled her. *'Who is this?'* Silas thought.

"It's not my wife, but a demon from hell," Mr. Hawthorne said, his voice cracking with emotion. He put a hand up to wipe away the tears that were there. "Now go on, lad. Faster." He stumbled after Silas as the woman followed along at their side.

"That's not true," the woman said. Her voice encircled them. In the red light, her skin seemed almost transparent. She was as white as the trees in the garden and her eyes were dark. Her fingernails were ragged and sharp as razors. "I'm your Belinda. I'm the one you married under the poplar trees by the winding brook. Ah, what a day that was. All of the riders in their fine wolf cloaks and the mist people came from miles around. Even Mrs. Deiva and her husband came from the house to watch. It was a celebration that lasted for days."

"Stop it, witch! Don't sully her name," Mr. Hawthorne said.

Silas looked back and gasped. The groundskeeper was staggering blind from the tears and was inches away from stepping off the path into the Shadow Garden.

"Mr. Hawthorne, watch where you're going," Silas said, slowing the wheelbarrow again.

Belinda hissed at him and turned back to her husband. "It was a celebration that lasted all the years of my life, through the birth of our daughter and many a planting."

"No more," Mr. Hawthorne said. "Leave me be."

"I tried to get you to leave. The three of us to go through the gates and start a new life, but you wouldn't do it, wouldn't leave behind the centuries your family took care of this forsaken land. Look at me now," Belinda said, posing in moonlight. Her jaws opened so wide Silas could no longer see her face, only a mouth with dozens of sharp, crooked teeth so that he wondered in amazement how she ever managed to keep from tearing her lips apart. "Do you like what the Smiling Ladies have made me?"

"No, no. It can't be," Mr. Hawthorne said. His cheeks were wet with tears. "I would have done

116

anything to help you."

"Except risk your own life," she said. A thick, red tongue rolled out of her mouth and waved in the air like an insect antenna.

"Cassandra, I had to think of Cassandra," he said.

"How is my daughter? Tell her that Mother can't wait to give her a kiss," Belinda said with a cold laugh.

Mr. Hawthorne stopped walking. He was standing feet away from crossing into the Shadow Garden. The woman who had been his wife was beckoning him to her with the claws that used to be her hands. As Silas watched, the groundskeeper took one, then two steps towards her.

"No!" Silas yelled. He dropped the wheelbarrow and it dumped over the earth and dead witch vines. He grabbed the groundskeeper and pulled him away from the garden. "Mr. Hawthorne, Mr. Hawthorne, please. Think of your daughter."

The groundskeeper looked as if he didn't know who Silas was, then recognition stirred in his eyes. "You're right, boy. It wouldn't be fair to Cassie. I'm tired, though. Sometimes a man gets so tired."

"Let's go," Silas said, lifting the wheelbarrow. "Everything looks better after a good night's sleep."

"You'll pay for this," the woman called as Silas and Mr. Hawthorne left the trail. "I'll feast on your sister's blood, you fool."

They were nearing the groundskeeper's cottage

before either of them spoke. "Best not bring this up around Cassandra, lad," Mr. Hawthorne said, tired-sounding. "It'll only upset her."

Silas was emptying the dead vines in a compost heap behind the barn when Osbold landed on his shoulder and nuzzled tenderly at him. In the past month, he and the little gargoyle had become fast friends. The same couldn't be said for Silas and the groundskeeper's daughter. If anything, she took a particular pleasure in insulting him and his family. The nicer he tried to be, the meaner it made her.

"There he is, old jelly-bean eyes," Cassandra said, coming around the barn with a smirk on her face. The different colors of his eyes were a favorite insult of hers. "Did you chip a nail helping with the planting?"

Silas thought of the thing in the Shadow Garden that had claimed to be Cassandra's mother and ground his teeth.

"You'll never guess where I spent my day," she said, leaning on the fence to watch him muck out the last of the wheelbarrow.

"No, but I imagine you'll tell me," he said.

"Fine, then. Since you asked, I spent the day with the lady of the manor, Lily Blackwood."

Silas stopped and looked at her. Cassandra had a pleased look on her face. "You saw Lily?"

"In the flesh. Not nearly as unpleasant as her brother. She invited me back again in two days."

"How — how was she?"

"As fine as anyone can be in her situation. She

told me to give you a message."

"Well, what is it?"

Cassandra ignored him. She put her hands behind her back and began to whistle while pretending to walk an invisible line so she could draw out his torment. When Silas wouldn't give her the satisfaction of an irritated look, she spoke. "Oh, all right. She said to tell you that she was fine and that she....," the groundskeeper's daughter paused as though she were going to vomit the word. "And to tell you that she loved you."

"And what did you tell her?" Silas sighed in relief that his sister was fine. Osbold rubbed his leathery skin against the side of Silas's head and picked at something in his hair.

"I wondered how a girl so beautiful could have such an odd-looking brother," Cassandra laughed. "Come on Osbold, let's leave the stable boy to finish his chores." She put out her arm and the gargoyle flew and perched on her arm.

"You'll tell her I'm fine as well?" he said.

"I'm not in the habit of being a messenger," she said. "It's lucky for you I'm in a good mood tonight."

'What did I do to make her hate me so?' Silas thought, as he approached the bunkhouse. A group of lathery horses were tied in front and he almost broke into a run when he saw his uncle's among them. It had been more than a month since Jonquil and the other men had headed into the mist and though none of the riders mentioned it, Silas could

tell they were nervous. "Not normal to be gone so long," he heard Larkspur say one night after he'd drank two flagons of wine. "We need to go after them." There were ayes from the other riders. Skuld banged his one good arm on the table hard enough that it rattled the wooden plates and cups. "If Jonquil's been gone so long it's because he's got a good reason." Silas almost told Skuld about the man he'd seen talking with the wolf that night, but at the last minute decided to keep it to himself. Which didn't mean the boy hadn't tried to figure out who it was. There were 32 riders in the bunkhouse. Seven of those Silas discarded instantly; they were old riders who couldn't do more than cook, keep up the camp, and talk about their glory days. Silas also discounted his uncle and the men with him, and that knocked the number down to 20 — still large, but more manageable. He was inclined to take Arfast and Skuld from the list as well, which made the number less. From there, he observed the remaining riders and their routines, trying to deduce the mysterious person, but with no luck. Silas slept lightly and watched who entered and left the bunkhouse, but whoever it was, he never repeated his journey into the woods.

Voices spilled from the bunkhouse in excitement as he approached. The front door was open and oily light fell on trampled mud in front of the barracks. A pair of dusk riders stood in the shadows watching the meadow for signs of anything approaching. Their wolf cloaks were filthy yellow and they clutched muskets to their chests.

"How long?" Silas asked, stepping onto the sagging porch.

"Nought as the crow flies," one of the riders said. "Came out of the mist as though they were being chased by the devil himself."

A scream of pain from inside the bunkhouse ripped the night, followed by the sound of someone shouting "Hold him down!" Silas moved towards the door and the rider blocked him.

"What are you doing?" Silas asked.

"It's your uncle, he —." Concern etched the rider's features. "He's hurt badly."

Silas pushed past the man and entered a bunkhouse that was scrambling with activity. Chaos reigned. Men were running back and forth. One rider was throwing boxes from a cupboard, wildly searching for something. Another collected herbs and potions from a dusty shelf. Three men lay on cots and were being forced to hold still. "They've gone mad with fever. Bring me water," Larkspur shouted. He was feeling the temperature of a rider whose face boiled red and eyes looked ready to pop from their sockets. Veins throbbed in the man's forehead and neck. Larkspur pushed him back down on the cot. "Hurry, he doesn't have much time."

Silas searched the room for his uncle. A group of riders huddled around a table deep in discussion.

Skuld was shouting. "Tell me what happened again. Blast it!" Silas saw Brayeur, one of the riders who went with his uncle, stretched out on a cot with a bandage over one eye. His skin was a sickly yellow and a rank odor poured from him. Brayeur couldn't have been more than thirty, but something had sapped his energy and he spoke as though it exhausted him. "I've told you, I don't know. We followed strange trails into the mist until we were lost. That was when the attack happened."

"And you didn't see what it was?"

The rider swallowed. "I caught only a glimpse."

"What did you see?"

"A man," he said.

"A man did this?" Skuld said, disbelieving.

"I don't know. I only saw him for an instant."

"What did he look like?"

"The mist plays strange tricks," Brayeur said.

"Tell me. Blast it," Skuld said. Across the room, one of the injured riders called out for his mother in a delirium.

Brayeur stared lost in memory, struggling to find the exact words to describe what had attacked them.

"I heard the screams before I saw him. We'd been traveling for days, through a mist thick enough to test a man's sanity. I could barely see the horse in front of me. We were past the villages, well into the area where the nothingness starts."

"Why would you go that deep? It's too easy to get lost and never find your way back," Skuld said in disbelief.

"We were tracking whatever was dragging the villagers from their homes and killing them. It was Jonquil who discovered the tracks beside the cabin. We found the bodies nearby, fresh dead — an old man and a little boy. They were — they were skinned alive, empty husks, all of the good stuff scooped out of them," The rider rocked back and forth at the terrible image.

"And you followed the trail?" Skuld said, trying to get the man back on track.

"Yes, deeper into the mist until everyone thought we were lost, but Jonquil wouldn't quit. Kept saying we were going to catch up with whatever it was. That we could stop the killing. And then, instead of us finding it, the creature found us."

Brayeur told Skuld how he'd heard screaming coming from the direction in which Jonquil had gone. The sound was strange in the blinding mist and had echoed from different directions until he was disoriented. His horse whinnied with fear and it took all his skill to calm it down. Somewhere to his right, a rider called out, "Stay back, I warn you," an explosion followed as a flintlock was fired. He pulled his own pistol and loosened the strap on his sword. Every rider was prepared for death, for they lived in its constant shadow at Nightfall Gardens, but that didn't mean any wanted to die. "Riders to me," Jonquil called from the fog, but Brayeur couldn't tell where his call had come from. Another shriek came from nearby and he gripped the gun tightly, his palm sweating. A body flew from the mist and landed close enough that he could tell it was Fenwick, one of the riders. His skin looked as though it'd been turned inside out; he was a mess of blood and gore. Brayeur spurred his horse forward and charged directly into the creature.

"What did he look like?" Skuld asked, more gently now that he'd heard the horrible story.

"He was seven feet tall. Aye, the tallest person I've ever seen and his arms were no bigger around than a whipping branch, but stronger than ten of us. His skin was hard as iron and sickly gray. His beard touched his knees and I saw live things moving inside of it. Whatever he was, I saw no eyes, only empty sockets where they used to be. A pair of antlers grew from his forehead and glistened with blood and poison," Brayeur shuddered at the ghastly memory.

Silas saw a flash of recognition cross Skuld's face, but one second later it was gone.

"And how'd you get out of that mess?" Skuld asked.

Brayeur laughed so hard that Silas thought the others were going to have to hold him down and force draught of the mina worm down his gullet to calm him. "My gun," he said, when he could continue. "I pulled the trigger and it backfired, blew me off my horse and near killed me. When I woke up, he was gone, one of the riders was dead and the others were torn and injured."

"And why would he leave without finishing the job?" Skuld asked.

"Who's to say he didn't? We're poisoned, can't you tell? It's searing our blood and killing us."

"What could do such a thing?" One of the riders asked Skuld.

"Eldritch," Skuld said after a long pause, and Silas felt fear go through the room at the name. Several of the riders started muttering. "Couldn't be," one of the riders said. "Jonquil chased him into the nothingness. No one has ever come back from that."

Skuld frowned. "Then *no one* did a lot of damage to five of our best riders," he said. "If it's true he's back, then we're in more trouble than I thought."

Silas pushed out of the group and saw Arfast helping tend one of the wounded riders. "Where's Jonquil?" he asked, looking for his uncle.

The young rider looked up at him as he cleaned a gash on the rider's chest. The warmth and humor that was normally there was gone. "No lies, little one. He's injured something fierce," Arfast said.

Silas gasped when he realized his uncle was spread out on the cot in front of him. Jonquil's face was shriveled and the color was drained from him. Even his lips were white. Sweat beaded on his forehead as he burned with fever. He was so ghostly looking that Silas was surprised when his chest heaved to draw breath. Jonquil's mouth moved as if he were trying to speak.

"What's wrong with him?" Silas asked.

"The poison has worked its way deep. It's powerful dark, from the times when the old gods walked. Nothing works against it," Arfast said. As if to prove his point, he poured blue liquid from a vial on the wound and Jonquil thrashed with madness as it turned from aqua to bubbling black. "It's too strong."

"What about Mr. Hawthorne and his spell box?" Silas asked.

"A rider is already on his way to him. Pray he knows what he's doing," Arfast said. "Because if he doesn't, there's nothing else to be done. This will kill them all before long."

Silas's heart dropped. He'd just met his uncle, and while he couldn't say he exactly liked him, Jonquil held a great many answers about this place and no matter what, he was still family.

Across the room, one of the injured riders thrashed and screamed, trying to push off the men who were holding him down. "Watch your uncle," Arfast said. "I'm going to help them." His cloak swept behind him as he turned to help the others subdue the man.

Silas thought of his play, the one he'd left at the Golden Bough when he'd decided to save his sister. The monsters he'd conjured in his head for that play were nothing compared to the terror that they faced here every day. He touched Jonquil's boiling forehead and his uncle's hand shot out, grabbing his wrist hard enough he thought it was going to snap. His uncle's eyes opened and stared right through him.

"Thomas?" Jonquil said. His voice was shaky with fever.

"It's Silas, your nephew," Silas tried to pull his hand away. The grip was locked so hard he couldn't move.

Jonquil's eyes cleared for a brief second. "Silas? Of — of course. Where am I?"

"You're at the bunkhouse," Silas said.

"My men?" his uncle asked.

"They're okay," Silas lied.

Relief flooded Jonquil's eyes. "That's good. It was my mistake. Didn't realize what it was until -." He started to fade and then came back. "It's starting."

"What is?"

"I didn't realize how close they've come. How long they've planned," his uncle said.

"Who? What are you talking about?" Silas leaned closer. He could smell the sickness radiating from Jonquil. If Mr. Hawthorne wasn't able to help, none of them would last long.

"No time," Jonquil said in a ragged whisper. "Don't trust anyone. There are traitors in our midst."

"Who?" Silas asked, but it was too late. His uncle collapsed from exhaustion as the fever ravaged him. The door opened and the groundskeeper came in, his shirt collar undone, hauling his spell box. "Where are they?" he said.

"Everyone clear back and let me get to work."

Only later, when he was safely in bed, would Silas ponder his uncle's words and the ill omens they held for Nightfall Gardens.

9
Lily Sees Her Death

The wallpaper was moving. That was the first thing Lily noticed when she entered the room following Abigail. Stories were weaving themselves on the ochre-colored wallpaper. Intricately detailed shapes were coming into existence.

'Where is she?' Lily thought. Her aunt had vanished and left her alone in this abandoned room. A candle burning on a nearby roll-top writing desk and a battered wardrobe in one corner were the only other furniture there.

The shapes continued to draw themselves on the walls. Lily stepped closer to watch. She saw a creature with the head of a snake and body of a human whipping a group of people who fell on their knees in worship. On another wall, witches warmed a pot for dinner while children locked inside a cage screamed for help. In a different scene, a dragon with scales so detailed that they formed ten thousand diamonds flew over a village, burning it to the ground. In yet another, a man was chained to a mountainside as vultures feasted on his flesh. Scenes of horror, too many to comprehend, passed before her eyes. Night creatures came forth to drag families from their beds. Goblins made slaves of humans. The old gods walked the earth and destroyed with no thought of the lives they were taking. The images shifted and changed on the walls, like some magic lantern show of terror that played over and over again. Lily's stomach tightened and she felt she was going to be sick. *'Abigail wanted me to see this. Wanted me to understand what was at stake. This was what the world was like before Prometheus trapped all of the evil inside the box'* she thought, watching as a tentacled creature came from the depths of the ocean and pulled a ship under the waves. Tears stung her eyes as a young girl, much like herself, was chased through dark woods by wolves. The girl came to a cliff and jumped into a ravine rather than be torn apart by their jaws. The scenes continued. This was what her ancestor had almost unleashed on the world. This was why Lily was here. She shuddered at the thought of all of these things free to roam the world. Once they were loose, there would be no more theater, no more Paris, New Amsterdam, or anything. The world as she knew it would cease to exist and countless people would die. All because of her. *'No,'* she thought. *'It's not my fault. I* shouldn't have to pay for a mistake that a relative made centuries ago. It's not fair.' Lily ran her hands along her goose-bumped arms. More images and stories unfolded, each more ghastly than the one before. Monsters with claws and fangs made sport of the humans they caught. Gigantic worms burst from the ground and swallowed homes. Malignant spirits drove people to the brink of madness and beyond. "Enough," Lily said, putting her hands over her eyes, only to discover that they were wet with tears. "Enough, please make it stop." But still, the images didn't end. She turned to flee, and that was when a drawer on the writing desk slid open.

Lily didn't want to look inside, but she couldn't shake the feeling that she'd been brought here for some other reason than to be reminded of her family history. She got the candle from the table and brought it close. A slim journal was lying in the drawer. Lily removed the book and shut the drawer. *Abigail Blackwood* was stitched onto the cover. She tucked it under her arm and looked once more at the walls. Now an end scene was playing out, where all the evils were being pulled inside a box being held by a man that could only be Prometheus. Lily watched for a moment more and left the room.

Back in the safety of her bed, Lily opened the moldering book. On the first page was a map of the house with different rooms and floors penciled in with various colors. Several rooms had X's drawn across them. *'I'm not sure how useful this is, since the house is constantly changing,'* she thought. Still, the main hall and kitchen were in the same place, and she saw other rooms such as the library, a solarium, and an in-door swimming pool, that she didn't know existed. Passageways lined the walls behind some rooms, including Abigail's bedroom where Lily was now. She got up and knocked on the walls until she heard a hollow sound. It didn't surprise her that a house so alive as Nightfall Gardens should be full of secret passages connecting different floors the way arteries controlled the flow of blood to the heart. Still, when her fingers found a notch in the woodwork and pressed it, she cried out when the wall slid back with a groan, revealing a cobwebbed opening.

Wind sucked at her candle flame. She smelled stale air and something rotten coming from inside. Far off, Lily heard pipes knocking and scuttling sounds like fingers tapping on bricks. After the night's festivities, she wanted nothing more than to crawl into bed. Instead, she swept the cobwebs aside and entered the passage. A chill crept down her back. Candlelight reflected pale yellow from the stone of the corridor until it was swallowed by darkness. A breeze ruffled her hair and blew through the passage. She took one and then two tentative steps, the candle held in front of her for protection. The knocking grew louder the farther she went. It was an urgent, rhythmic banging that sounded like a boiler about to explode. The scuttling sound was there as well, buried underneath. One second it was a whisper at her ear, the next it sounded as though it were coming from above. Ahead, two shafts of light penetrated the passage. *'Where's that coming from?'* she thought. Lily stood on tiptoe and found herself looking through the eyeholes of a painting into an extravagant music room. Red moonlight fell on gilt-edged wallpaper and a grand piano. A golden harp that looked beautiful enough for the gods themselves to pluck was next to the piano. None of that was what caught her attention, though: a man wearing a powdered wig, a yellow coat, and high breeches with buckled shoes was pacing the room. He sat down at the piano, cracked his knuckles as if about to play and then shoved violently away from it and began pacing again. He did this once, twice, three times. Right then, the man turned toward the painting as if he knew he was being observed and rushed towards her. In that brief instant she saw that his face was nothing more than decomposing flesh over a long dead body.

Lily stepped away from the painting and forced herself to stifle a scream. The knocking from the pipes grew louder and the scuttling seemed almost at her feet. She waited a long moment and still shaking, peered back into the room and found herself staring into a pair of red rimmed eyes that shifted from side to side and stared out at her. Lily ran back toward her room. *'I've had enough excitement for tonight,'* she thought as she fled down the passage. The knocking grew more distant and she saw light spilling from the opening to her room. Only then did she realize that the scuttling sound was following her and seemed to be growing louder. *'What is—'* Lily got no farther with her thought. A spider the size of a small kitten was hanging from the side of the wall. Its fangs were dripping venom that smoked as it hit the floor and its eight black eyes reflected candlelight. Red stripes ran along its back. It made a chattering sound as it came at her.

Lily moved with the reflexes of someone who was exhausted and angered with nothing to lose. She thrust the candle at the spider and it recoiled from the flame and sprang to the floor, its front legs clicking like hands rubbing together at a juicy prize. Lily's one overriding desire was to get in her room and shut the door on this nightmare. The opening was right behind her. She could see her bed and Abigail's open diary lying on top of the covers. But the spider wasn't going to let her go that easy now that its prey was in sight. A strand of silk shot from the underside of the arachnid into her face. Lily ripped at it as the silk began to harden and suffocate her. At the same moment, the spider charged her exposed legs, chirping in victory. This time, she did scream. She thrust the candle at it again, but the spider didn't slow down. As Lily backed into her room, she felt for the notch that controlled the secret door. The door groaned and began to swing shut as the spider appeared. Its legs waved in the air and it danced with triumph.

"Get — out — of — my — room," Lily shouted, and now she was angry, angrier than she had been since the glass dolls attacked her. She drove the spider back with the flame, coming so close that the spider let out a screech when it touched the hot wax. Lily thrust the candle at it again and this time the spider hesitated. It didn't notice the door swinging shut until the last second when it made a desperate plunge back toward its home. It wasn't fast enough, though. Lily saw the spider trapped in the closing door and then it was gone, leaving behind nothing but a pair of pencil-sized legs. She put her head to the wall and thought she heard screeching on the other side as she collapsed on the floor in exhaustion.

Ursula was the one who found her the next morning. "Rough one last night, my lady? I've had plenty of those, I have. Me old mom used to say there's nothing that can't be solved by a hot glass of lizard pus. Madam Deiva might frown on that though, so this steaming cider will have to do for ya."

As usual, Lily felt an unbearable depression weigh down on her whenever the housemaid was around. Tears stung her eyes as she thought of the night before and the misery of her life. "There, there, miss. It's going to be another overcast day with a chance of thunderstorms. You can't ask for better than that," the housemaid said and waggled her unibrow at Lily.

Only after Ursula had cleaned her chamber and

was gone did Lily begin to feel like her old self. She took Abigail's diary and went down to the cavernous dining room, where she waited for Ozy to bring her morning tea and biscuits. She saw him several minutes before he got to the table, balancing a silver tray in his shaking hands. Lily had asked him once if he needed help and he had given her a look that could have curdled milk. She'd never asked again.

As she waited, Lily flipped through the book and was frustrated to find that everything was written in a nonsensical code of pyramids, waves and zeros. It was no language she recognized. *'Abigail must not have wanted the wrong person to get their hands on this book,'* Lily thought. She turned back to the map of the house; on the next page was a map of the gardens. The Labyrinth, Shadow and White Gardens were all there, as well as the mist land that tapered off into nothingness. The map showed the entrances and exits to the gardens. In addition, tunnels extended from the house into the center of each. *'Why would they want access from the house to the Gardens?'* Lily thought. She was pondering this when Ozy finally arrived with breakfast.

"Good morning, madam," the ancient butler said, taking a minute to place the shaking tray on the table. Lily fought the urge to snatch it from his hands in impatience. Ozy poured her a cup of tea; his hands trembled so badly it sloshed over the top of the cup onto the table. From this close, Lily could see through the wisps of his ginger hair to the parchment-colored skin beneath. Liver spots the size of birds' eggs crowned his skull. The butler's lips were a thin slit and dust plumed from his mouth. The ancient bandages he was wrapped in poked out around the neck and sleeves of the suit. What purpose they served, Lily had no idea. *'How much he must have seen and how many Blackwoods he must have served,'* she thought, spooning sugar into her tea. An idea came to her.

"Ozy, how many years have you been here?" she asked, taking the first sip of hot tea.

The butler paused as though no one had asked him a question in a very long time. Lily could almost hear him thinking behind the faded brown of his eyes. When he spoke it was a voice that sounded full of sawdust. "Seven — no — eight generations of your family. Before that I was there," he gestured with emaciated fingers towards the outside.

"The gardens?" Lily asked.

"The White Garden, my lady. I was a vengeance spirit meant to protect the tombs of one of the ancient pharaohs from looters and others who would do it harm."

"You were a mummy?" she said, intrigued.

Ozy stiffened as though insulted. "I would never use such a base word to describe us. That description was the product of some overactive writer's imagination. I prefer the term death warrior."

"But you're basically a mummy," Lily said, trying not to snicker. "So why are you no longer a — death warrior."

"Are you sure this is appropriate conversation for morning tea?" Ozy said. "I'm positive that, if I still had a digestive tract, it would upset my stomach."

Lily bit into a crumpet. "No, go ahead. That is, if you don't mind telling me."

"It's not a long story, madam," he said. "Many creatures of the Gardens are pure products of evil or malignity, who want nothing more than to harm or enslave those who are weaker than they are. Others are there by no fault of their own, only the unfortunate accident of their birth. I was one of the latter. Even when I walked the pyramids, I questioned what I was doing. I didn't have the violent nature of my kind. I learned that the hard way." Ozy stopped as though transported back into an ancient memory.

"What happened?" Lily asked, pouring herself another cup of tea.

"A young child snuck into the tomb one day looking for the hidden treasure that was there. I came upon him in one of the chambers as he cleared it of all the gold and silver inside. It was my job to torture him unto death, but when he turned around, I saw the truth."

"What was that?"

"That he was scared and hungry and was only stealing from the pyramid to feed his younger brother and sister who were starving in a nearby village."

"What did you do?" Lily asked.

"Why, I let him go. When the other death warriors found out what had happened, they were furious and sentenced me to a century of suffering. From that point on, I was looking for a way out. I waited longer than I care to remember, until one day I found myself walking on a path and looking back into the White Garden. Who knows how long I was there or how I was able to free myself; the Gardens muddy the thinking of those trapped there. Luckily, I was discovered by one of your great-great-great-great-great-grandfathers and he was kind enough to have faith in me. All of the household staff are reformed evils from the gardens," he said.

Lily couldn't believe what she was hearing. "Polly and Ursula as well?"

"Oh my, yes. There's no place for us in the outside world, so we stay here serving the Blackwood family."

It sounded like a sad existence, but Lily kept that to herself. "And you knew my father and mother?"

"Master Thomas was rebellious. He and Miss Moira thought that if they fled, they could escape their past. They didn't understand that the past is not something you can escape. May I be excused now?"

"I have one more question," Lily said. "What

was my Great-Aunt Abigail like? What happened to her?"

Ozy smiled until the parchment on his face looked as if it might rip. "She was my favorite. Miss Abigail was the most intelligent of all the Blackwoods I've had the pleasure of knowing. She knew this house better than anyone. She believed that the box used to bind us all was hidden somewhere here."

"What was she going to do with it if she found it?" Lily asked.

"She thought there was a way to undo all of this and free her family and those of us seeking redemption. An old fairy tale, but she believed it quite emphatically."

"What about the others?"

"Her father and mother laughed at her. Miss Deiva was more concerned with chasing boys than paying attention to her."

"What happened on the day she disappeared?"

"Your great-aunt was like a ghost the last few weeks of her life. Always exploring the house, scribbling in a notebook she carried. Her mother warned her how deadly this house is, but she wouldn't listen. Many a Blackwood and servant have died here. In its way, Nightfall Manor is as deadly as the gardens outside. I saw her that morning, right here at this same table. 'I'm getting close, Ozy,' she told me. 'There's something I have to do first, but soon we'll be free, once and for all.' After breakfast, Miss Abigail left and I never saw her again."

Lily broke a biscuit in two and dipped it in her tea. "What do you think happened to her?"

"The house, madam. Something in the house got her," he said. "We scoured this place from top to bottom and couldn't find her." Ozy looked at the floor and Lily was surprised to see a tear in one corner of his eye. It must have been centuries since any liquid touched his dried skin. The butler backed away from the table. "I must go now to prepare the turning of your gran's room."

'If only I could understand this book,' Lily said, looking hopelessly at her great-aunt's coded journal. *'There must be someone who can read it.'* But who could she trust? If the journal contained clues about Pandora's Box, then it was a secret that needed to be guarded fiercely. It couldn't fall into the wrong hands.

Lily spent the rest of the day trying to make sense of the diary. She held it up to the windows in the sitting room to see if it was covered in secret ink, but nothing was there. Outside in the Shadow Garden, caped figures were building what looked like a stage in a clearing. She watched them for a while and then drew the symbols on paper and tried re-arranging them, but all that did was make her more confused.

In the late afternoon, Lily went in search of the library. She found the room, massive and gloriously jumbled with books. The walls soared a hundred feet high and were filled with countless dusty books. A skylight illuminated the collected history of the Blackwood family. Books were stacked in heaps on the floor waiting to be shelved. The room was filled with the musty but comforting smell of knowledge. *'Where do I start?'* She thought. Lily picked up a random book about herbology from one of the stacks. She put it down and pulled a book from a nearby shelf: *A Secret History of Sea Creatures.* Lily perused another book: *I, Banshee, the Autobiography of a Death Foretold."* Nothing there either. She spent the next two hours without discovering anything that would help untangle the mystery of her aunt's journal.

That evening, Lily went to call on her grandmother. If anyone might know what the journal meant, it would be Deiva. When she got to her door, though, Polly came out and looked at her with pity in her white eyes. "Your gran's feeling poorly today, she is. I'm afraid the gilirot's taking its toll. You'll have to come back tomorrow, my lady. Your gran needs rest."

Lily went to bed that night with a heavy feeling in her heart. Deiva wouldn't live much longer and then what would happen? Would she be chained to Nightfall Gardens forever, until the same fate awaited her?

The next morning she made sure to be up bright and early so she would be out of her room before Ursula arrived. After her morning tea, she took Abigail's journal to the sitting room to pour over it one more time. She was surprised when she looked out onto the Shadow Garden and saw the cloaked figures had finished building the stage and that a performance was about to take place. Lily placed the book on the table next to her, curious to see what was happening. An actor dressed in a red mask and red robes came onto the stage and gesticulated with his arms as though he were telling a story. A moment later, the play began. Lily pivoted the antique brass telescope toward the stage so she could get a better look at the action. A woman in a blue muslin dress capered on the stage, wearing a silver mask that covered her face. A young man in a black mask chased after her. Every time he tried to grab the girl, she danced out of reach. Another man, dressed in gold with a gold mask, entered on the opposite side of the stage. As soon as the girl in blue saw him, she flew to his side and they embraced in a long kiss. The man in black's shoulders sagged and he stalked off the stage in anger. That was the end of the performance.

The man in the red mask swept back on and put his hands out for the actors to take a bow. The three came to the edge of the platform and bowed low at the waist, yanking their masks away as they did. When they stood, Lily gasped. The woman was her mother Moira, the man in gold was her father Thomas and the man in black was her Uncle Jonquil.

Before she could react any further, two men in wolf cloaks dragged a girl onto the stage with her hands tied behind her back. An executioner, hooded in black, walked behind them. He carried a double-edged ax that looked sharp and heavy enough to cleave marble. The girl was hauled to a post where her head was placed on a block. Lily hadn't seen her face, but she didn't need to. She would have known the soft blue dress and white blond hair flowing around the girl's face anywhere. Didn't she see it everyday when she looked in the mirror? She was looking at herself. *'They are trying to frighten me,'* she thought. Still, Lily couldn't manage to take her eye away from the telescope. The executioner raised the girl's head so Lily was looking into her own tear-streaked face, and then he pulled his ax back. Lily closed her eyes as it came down. When she opened them seconds later, the stage had vanished as though nothing had ever been there.

"My father says the Shadow Garden is the worst of the three," Cassandra said, standing next to her. Lily had been so intently watching what was happening that she hadn't noticed the green girl arrive.

"Why?" Lily asked. The image of the executioner's ax coming down on her neck played again in her mind.

"It's the most deceitful and deadly, an inverted mirror of the world outside where all of the creatures from nightmares live. I'm to keep away from it at all cost and never walk past it at night. One of the many superstitions my father has. What did it show you?"

"My own death," Lily said.

Cassandra laughed. "Then you won't die. At least not today." The green girl snatched Abigail's diary from the table. "What's this, then?"

Lily grabbed for it, but Cassandra was already out of reach and flipping through the pages.

"My great aunt's diary," she said. "Give it back."

Cassandra frowned and handed it back to her. "Hopefully, you can make more sense out of it than I can."

"Not really," Lily said. "I've been trying to decipher it all day, but can't understand a word."

"Doesn't surprise me."

"Why?"

"Because it's protected by magic. I can feel it."

"You can feel magic?" Lily asked.

"It's one of the many things I can do. Why are you in such a rush to figure out what's inside here?"

Lily thought about holding back the truth but realized she had to trust someone and right now, she didn't have any better options than the green girl with yellow hair. She told her about how she'd chased her aunt's ghost and about the room where all the history of humankind played out on the walls. She finished by describing the secret passage and the spider she'd fought.

"I don't know what to do next," Lily said. "But if there's a chance Abigail was right and we can close Pandora's Box, we have to try."

The gardener's daughter walked over and sat on the windowsill. The Shadow Garden was empty below. "I've never considered a life without Nightfall Gardens, where my father and I wouldn't know constant death or danger. I'm not even sure Osbold and I could fit in out there."

"You could come with us," Lily implored.

"And be freaks in a sideshow?" Cassandra said angrily.

"Maybe one of our doctors could cure you," Lily said.

"There's nothing wrong with me," Cassandra snapped.

"Of course," Lily said. "I only meant you could travel to London and Paris with me."

"What's that?"

"The grandest cities on earth," Lily said. "More amazing than Nightfall Gardens and far less deadly."

"I doubt that. Anyway, you're the one that dreams of being a fancy lady with fineries," Cassandra said. "I could never leave my father. What would he do without me? He's half-crazy since my mother died when I was a baby."

"How did she die?" Lily asked gently.

Cassandra's eyes narrowed. "I don't know you that well, Blackwood. I'd ask you to mind your own business before you pry into others'."

"I didn't mean —."

"Your lot never mean to," Cassandra said. Her

shoulders sagged as though recalling a painful memory. "All you need to know is my mother died when I was a wee bairn. I never knew her."

"I'm sorry," Lily said.

With that, the green girl picked up Abigail's diary and thumbed through it again. "Well, we'd better get started."

"Doing what?"

"You don't think I would sit idle if there was a chance to close this place once and for all? What would happen to the world if all of this evil came spilling back in to it? Your precious Paris would be no more. Not everyone is as selfish as you," Cassandra said.

"I don't know where to start," Lily said.

"We start by finding out what kind of magic is protecting this book and then we figure out a way to read what's inside."

"How do we do that?"

"By visiting Raga," Cassandra said.

"Who's Raga?"

"A person who can understand any form of magic. If she's not in one of her trances, she can tell us what type of spell has been put on this book and what we need to do to unlock its mysteries."

"Every door in this house is watched to make sure I don't go outside," Lily said exasperated. "How do you expect to get me past them?"

Cassandra smiled. Her teeth gleamed white against her green skin. "You did say something about secret passages to the outside, didn't you?"

10
Arfast and the Firedog

There were no such things as seasons in Nightfall Gardens. Summer didn't hearken in long sunny days. Fall didn't mean the changing of the leaves to fiery autumnal colors. Winter didn't bring cold or snow. Spring didn't herald rebirth or the renewal of the lands. Every day was the same — dismal, gray, and overcast.

Jonquil warned them that the sun never came to Nightfall Gardens. "Enjoy it while you can," he'd said. "For once we're inside you won't feel sunshine again until the next time the gate opens." Silas hadn't known how true his uncle's words were. Three months with no sun and the boy's skin was the color of alabaster. Silas found the lack of light affected him in other ways as well. He was moodier and more prone to serious thoughts. Some days when he worked the grounds with Mr.

Hawthorne, he thought he'd go mad if he looked up and saw the dark, bruised sky perpetually heavy with rain.

"How do you stand it?" he asked one day. "A person can learn to stand anything if they have to put up with it long enough," the groundskeeper replied. "There's some who go off their rockers after a while, like Mad Abraham, a dusk rider who rode his horse into the Labyrinth one day and never returned. Usually, when this happens, people leave as soon as the gates open and go far enough that this place is only a nightmare in their sleep. Me? I don't mind it though. It's the infernal heat I don't like."

It had been a month since the riders returned and still Jonquil wavered between life and death. Mr. Hawthorne gave the wounded riders a serum made from Devil's Claw and tended them with healing poultices as best he could, but the other riders including Brayeur had slipped away quietly over the past weeks and now only his uncle was left, sweating out toxins, while Skuld was in charge of the dusk riders. Silas sat with Jonquil every evening, telling him about his day. Sometimes his uncle babbled and raved about something in the mist and once he thought Silas's mother was there. "Moira, I'm sorry. Why'd you leave? I could never tell you. I wouldn't do that to Thomas."

"It'd be a right favor if someone put him out of his misery," Larkspur said one evening over a fire as the flames reflected yellow off of his eyebrows and beard. He lifted a tankard of ale and poured it down his mouth and the front of his shirt. "Eldritch poison rots to the core. It turns blood black and burns a person alive until they are roasted like a pig."

"What do you suggest we do then?" another rider called out.

"Only what Jonquil would do for us. Put him out of his misery," Larkspur said.

Silas lay in his bed, eyes closed, prepared to jump up and battle anyone that would injure his uncle.

"That's enough," Skuld said, emerging from the shadows. "If anyone can survive, it'll be him. I won't hear anymore of that talk while the Gardens are more alive than I've ever seen them."

"I'll hold my peace for now, One Arm," Larkspur said kicking his chair into the wall where it smashed to splinters. A group of riders jumped up with their hands on sword hilts and turned to face Skuld. "We were all close to Jonquil. But if there comes a time he's no longer the man he once was, neither you or anyone else will stop me from doing what's right."

"Let me guess who the leader of the dusk riders would be then?" Skuld said. He loosened the leather straps of the ax at his side.

"I'm honored you think so highly of me," Larkspur said. "For I'd certainly make a better leader than a man who got his arm gnawed off by a wolf."

"Your belly makes a big target," Skuld said. "It'll be hard for you to laugh with your guts spilling on the ground."

"I wonder how you'll scratch your nose with your other arm gone," the giant said, tapping his fingers on his sword handle.

Silas sat up, letting the blankets slip off him and yanking out the dagger he carried for protection. The dusk riders were forming into groups: those who supported Skuld and those who backed Larkspur. The two men were nose to nose with hatred in their eyes. If something didn't happen soon, there was no telling where it would end. As if someone could read his mind, the flames from the fire shot up as if gasoline had been poured on them and a firedog shot from the chimney. The dog was the size of a Labrador retriever and was made entirely of flames that crackled from its body. It bounded from the fire with a growl and lit up the room with its glow.

"What kind of trickery?" shouted one of the riders. He snatched at his sword and took a swing at the dog as it leaped on all fours and barked at the riders, racing in circles around the room. The rider's sword swept through the dog and it raised one leg, flames squirting from its underside, catching his pants on fire. The rider beat at his breeches and poured a jug of water on himself to extinguish the flames.

The firedog raced around the room, jumping from bed to bed while the riders tried to catch it. It barked and yipped and wagged its tail. The dog had no eyes, only the ever-shifting fire that seemed to give it shape.

"Come here, pooch," Larkspur said, getting in the way of the dog. "You wouldn't hurt your old friend, would you?"

"I'd be careful or your breath could burn this whole place down," Skuld said.

"Once I've settled this witchery, I'll settle you," Larkspur said. He leapt at the dog as it passed, but missed and crashed through a table. His massive bulk upended ale tankards and sent dirty dishes flying.

"Is that your plan?" Skuld said with a smirk. "Destroy all the furniture in here and he'll have no place to hide?"

Larkspur wiped gruel from his face and propped himself on an elbow. "If you've got a better suggestion, I'd like to see it."

"I'll show you how a trueborn dusk rider handles such mischief," Skuld said, stalking toward the firedog that was now chewing on firewood in front of the chimney.

Silas looked about the room at the tattered group watching with amusement. It was then that he noticed Arfast at the back of the crowd. The young trickster was cupping a ball of flame that he juggled from one hand to the other. Every time he moved his hands, the firedog moved with him. As he watched, Arfast looked over at him and winked. The trickster opened his hands and blew out the flame, as Skuld was preparing to cleave the firedog with his ax. Nothing remained of it but the smell of brimstone.

"It ran in fear, did you see that?" Skuld said thumping his chest.

Larkspur retrieved a wine pouch from the floor where he lay. He laughed. "Is that what you call it? It seemed to me it left at its own leisure."

"Mayhap I should buy you a pair of spectacles the next time the gates open," Skuld said.

The giant flashed a wine-stained grin and the tension drained from the room as the riders took to cleaning the broken table and discussing what had occurred. While this was happening, Silas saw Arfast disappear out of the bunkhouse into the night. He slipped on his boots and followed.

The red moon hung so low overhead that Silas felt sure that if he reached up he could touch it. Heavy rainclouds scuttled across the sky, buoyed by high winds. The mist crept across the dew-covered meadow towards the bunkhouse. Silas thought he saw flashing yellow eyes inside the shrouded fog and then they were gone. Arfast was striding towards the gardens fast enough that he had to jog to catch up with him. The rider stopped near an ancient Maidenhair Tree that was close to the entrance of the Labyrinth. Bushes that were twenty feet tall marked the barrier of the garden. They ran along until they disappeared into the fog. Unlike the other Gardens, there was no way inside the labyrinth without going through the entrance.

Silas listened to see if he could hear anything coming from inside, but all he heard was the sound of wind blowing against leaves.

Arfast grabbed hold of the gnarled trunk of the tree and swung himself onto the lowest branch. He turned back and smiled at Silas. "Well, what are you waiting for? Are you going to climb with me or not?"

With those words, the young rider began pulling himself from one branch to the next until the only thing that could be seen was the white of his wolf's cloak. Silas looked toward the distant lights of the bunkhouse and grabbed the knotted bark, following after. He felt the sap under his fingers and the sting of pine needles as he shimmied up the branches. His face was streaked with sap by the time he came to the limb where Arfast sat with his feet dangling over the side. From here, they could see the length of Nightfall Manor and over the three gardens to where the world ended in a blur of fog. Something snorted in the Labyrinth and Silas thought he saw a horned figure with a human chest hurtle down one of the pathways and away into the maze. Paths zigzagged and crisscrossed leading in different directions inside the Labyrinth. It would be easy to get lost there and wander until you died of starvation or went mad, he thought. Who knew what resided inside the puzzle path. "All of the old gods that existed and those who are to come," Mr. Hawthorne told him once.

"That was a neat trick with the firedog," Silas said.

"I picked that up from the mist people," Arfast said. "Those two seemed in no mood to listen to reason, so I came up with a way to stop them."

"Larkspur was going to kill my uncle," Silas said.

Arfast cut a small branch from the tree and began whittling. "Easier said than done. He'd never have been so bold if Jonquil wasn't sick. Even now, your uncle has more friends than any man in the bunkhouse. If Skuld hadn't stopped him, someone would."

A light flashed in one of the rooms of Nightfall Manor and Silas saw his sister very clearly. Lily was standing at the window looking out at the wild tangle of gardens were he was hid. 'She can't see you,' Silas thought. 'You're out here with all the beasts that would do her harm.' A great feeling of tenderness welled up inside of him for her, locked in the strange house with no company except for the housekeepers, their dying grandmother, and Cassandra, the green girl, who was filled with some great rage. He watched until the light turned off and the manor was quiet once more.

"My sister," Silas said.

"Aye, she looks out that window every night before she goes to sleep," Arfast said.

Silas felt a momentary flicker of irritation that the rider hadn't brought him here until this night. "Spying on her, are you?"

"You couldn't blame me if I did," Arfast said grinning. "But no, this Maidenhair is the highest point in the Gardens. I like to come here and keep a lookout on things. Sometimes its almost peaceful."

"How'd you end up here?" Silas asked. The red moon was obscured for a moment as a blanket of clouds covered it, leaving them in near total darkness. Arfast's face and wolf cloak were all he could make out in the dark.

"I was drawn here, same as the others," Arfast said, and Silas heard the sound of his knife shaving wood in the dark. "Nightfall Gardens calls to those who listen, but very few find their way here. Fewer still live long after they arrive."

"Do you have family out there?" Silas asked, thinking of Thomas and Moira.

"I have a mother who loves me and a father who would kill me if he ever laid eyes on me again," Arfast said.

"What did you do?" Silas asked. The clouds drifted away and the red moon was back. Its light spilled like blood upon Arfast who had whittled the branch to splinters.

"What I had to. My father was a small man with a great temper that he took out on my mother and myself. He was quick with a bow or compliment to our landowner, but to those who loved him, he was violent and cruel. He believed the world was cheating him out of his share and was full of envy at those with more. If someone had wealth, he coveted it. If someone's wife was prettier or child was better behaved, he wished ill upon them. He was a coward with everyone but his family and blamed us for all of his bad luck. My mother, a timid kindly woman, was most often the one to receive the brunt of his fists, especially as I grew older, for he became fearful of me. 'Don't stare that way, boy,' he used to say, after he'd thrashed my mother for dropping a plate or forgetting to sweep the hearth. 'She asked for it. One day you'll understand.' I bided my time and waited until the chance came to pay him back for what he'd done." The trickster's voice dropped to a whisper and it seemed as if the whole Garden was listening to the sad tale.

"What did you do then?" Silas asked.

"A horrible evil," Arfast said. "One that I've spent these many years regretting. One that drew me to the Gardens to pay my penance."

A wolf howled in the mist. It was followed by a return call from somewhere in the Gardens.

"I came from fishing the stream behind our house and found my mother on the floor. Her face was battered and she could barely open her eyes, they were so swollen. My father was standing over her, yelling about a goat that had escaped from its pen. Something that was his fault, not hers. A wild rage overtook me and I grabbed a boiling pot from the fire and flung it into his face. He screamed as the bubbling liquid burned his flesh and ran into the doorway, trying to make his escape. I helped my mother to her feet and went to find him. He hadn't gone far. He couldn't. The scalding liquid burned him so badly that it blinded him. His eyes were burst eggs in their sockets."

Silas was at a loss for words. The story was more horrible than he'd imagined. "What happened after that?" he asked finally.

"I stayed until my father learned to live in his new sightless world. Neither he nor my mother ever forgave me. I can't say I blame them. When I was sure that they were able to get by, I ran away. They no longer wanted me there and he could no longer hurt her. I wandered the mountains for many months until I began to dream of this place."

Arfast followed the signposts in those dreams until he arrived one afternoon at the gates of Nightfall Gardens, a filthy boy covered in rags. "I walked through them and your uncle was the first to greet me. I've never regretted my decision. We're the ones that protect the world from the evils slumbering here."

The trickster finished his story and clambered down the tree. When he and Silas were on the ground, Arfast wiped his hands on his breeches. After the last few nights of restlessness, the gardens seemed unusually quiet. The smell of bittershade carried on the wind from nearby.

"Why'd you bring me here?" Silas asked. "I know it wasn't to tell your story."

Arfast's face was devoid of the good humor it usually carried. "We have to save Jonquil. If someone as lazy and gluttonous as Larkspur should take charge of the riders, this whole place will be in trouble."

"Wouldn't Skuld be next in command?" Silas asked. "My uncle placed him in charge before he left for the mist lands."

"It doesn't work that way. When the dusk rider leader passes, a vote is taken for who will be the next in charge. It's a popularity contest, not who would actually do the best job. Skuld is crafty but dour. He wouldn't stand a chance against a backslapper like Larkspur."

"What can we do, then? The Eldritch poison is eating away at my uncle. Nothing Mr. Hawthorne gives him does more than slow it for a little while," Silas said.

"And nothing he can give him will. Eldritch poison always kills. The cure for what ails Jonquil can only be found in one place."

"Where?"

"There's the danger," Arfast said. "Fairy Bells only grow inside the White Garden."

"Fairy Bells?"

"The milk from this plant can cure any ill, but only once. It's guarded by Cerberus, the guardian of the underworld— A nasty three-headed dog that consumes the blood of the living and makes sure that none escape to live again."

Silas wanted to laugh. It sounded absurd, but then he thought of the Shade that had pretended to be his sister to draw him into the White Garden. Mr. Hawthorne had warned him never to leave the path and enter the gardens themselves.

"How would we survive in the White Garden? As soon as we set foot in there, wouldn't the spirits be on us? Even if we endured that, how would we find our way to where these Fairy Bells grow? And then how would we get past this flesh-eating three-headed dog you're talking about?"

"I have my ways," Arfast said. "But if you're not up to the challenge, we could let your uncle continue to waste away until he dies and Larkspur is made head of the dusk riders."

They crossed the dew-covered field toward the bunkhouse. Inside, they heard the raucous sound of the riders drinking and making merry. Arfast and Silas nodded at the stone-faced sentry and entered to find a group gathered around Larkspur as he drained another calfskin of wine and told them a bawdy story.

"I said, I'd rather sleep on a feather bed, but this'll do just fine," the giant said, telling the punchline of a joke. The riders broke into laughter around him. Skuld sat away from the merriment and watched through slitted eyes. Silas saw this and realized what a disaster it would be if Larkspur were in charge of leading the men. *'They'll fall apart in months,'* he thought. *'And then who will protect Lily?'*

"How do we do this?" Silas said to Arfast.

The trickster grinned. "There's the old Blackwood spirit. Meet me tomorrow afternoon when the crow flies at the Stone Circle and we'll ready ourselves to enter the White Garden."

Silas slept with a troubled mind, dreaming of the spirits of the White Garden tearing at his flesh. When he woke early the next morning, he felt exhausted and splashed a cold pail of water over his head to clear his thoughts. Only a handful of the riders were up and about; most were still too drunk from last night's revelry to be up yet. Skuld and a small group were about to make their morning rounds when he came onto the porch.

"Have you ever seen such a sorry lot," Skuld said. "Your uncle would've had them on patrol by now. I'd drag 'em out myself, but Larkspur says I have no claim to do so and an extra couple of hours of sleep will hurt no one. We'll see how he feels when this place falls, the fool." With that, the one-armed man turned and rode away toward the Shadow Garden.

Silas happened on a strange sight when he approached the Hawthornes' cottage not long afterward. As he walked toward the front door to meet the groundskeeper, he heard sobbing coming from the side of the house.

"Mr. Hawthorne?" Silas asked. When he heard no response, he went around the side of the house and almost walked into Cassandra, who was standing over a dead rabbit. Tears streaked her green face. Osbold was perched on her shoulder cooing while nipping gently at her ear.

"Are you all right?" he asked reaching out to touch her arm. Cassandra jumped as though she'd been touched with a hot poker. "What do you want, ugly boy?" she said, lashing out at him.

Silas was overwhelmed by the rage coming from her. He looked at the brown rabbit lifeless on the ground. There were no marks or signs of wrong doing upon it. The green girl wiped away the tears in her eyes.

"I — I'm sorry. I heard you crying. Was — was that your pet?" He asked.

"My father brought it to me the last time the gates were open. It chewed through its rabbit hutch somehow. I was trying to catch it."

"How did it die?" Silas asked puzzled.

Cassandra rubbed her hands together in nervousness. "I don't know. All I did was —." She caught herself. "It — it just fell over before I could do anything."

"Can I look?" Silas asked. He got down on his knees and turned the rabbit over. The last of its warmth was fading even as he stroked the fur looking for injury.

Cassandra regained her composure. Osbold flew from her shoulder onto the roof of the cottage, where the gargoyle walked along the gutter on the roof. "Maybe you should mind your own business," she said.

Silas stood and wiped his hands on his pants. "I was only trying to help."

"The same as you're helping your sister," she said with a wicked sneer to her face.

The comment stung and anger bubbled inside of

him. "What do you know of my sister?"

"More than you think. While you're playing at being a rider, she's trying to find a way out of this place," she said.

"What are you talking about?"

Before Cassandra could reply, Mr. Hawthorne ambled around the side of the house. "I thought I heard your voice," he said to Silas. "You ready to finish digging that irrigation ditch?"

The groundskeeper looked down and saw the dead rabbit on the ground. "Oh Cassie, what happened. What have you done?"

While Silas was puzzling over Mr. Hawthorne's words, Cassandra began crying again. "I didn't mean to. I was trying to put him back in his hutch. I barely touched him." Tears streamed down her face. She took off charging towards the mist. Osbold flew from his perch and followed her into the shifting whiteness that enveloped the nearby woods.

Mr. Hawthorne stared pensively at the ground. "She'll be all right," he said. "I've warned her about touching living things."

"What does that mean?" Silas asked. He thought of how Cassandra jumped away from his touch.

"Nothing to concern yourself with, lad," Mr. Hawthorne said. "Let's bury this rabbit and then we have a full day of work ahead of us. We need to finish the irrigation ditch and plant more Dragonbreath flowers around the house. They're dying more quickly than they should. Miss Deiva must be growing weak indeed."

Silas threw himself into the rest of the day with such energy that there was little time to think of anything else. He and Mr. Hawthorne finished the ditch by afternoon and then went to work on planting a new bed of Dragonbreath flowers. Two thoughts preyed on his mind: the dead rabbit and Cassandra, and Arfast and the White Garden. *'I don't know why I should care about her anyway,'* he thought of Cassandra. He pushed that to the back of his mind for later. For now, he could only worry about the challenge that lay ahead of him.

When the sky turned from numbing gray to dark, he set off toward the Shadow Garden. A strange quietness hung over everything, like the expectation before a massive storm arrives. The stone circle was a meeting place for the Blackwoods so old that no one remembered its purpose anymore. It was built in a clearing between the Shadow Gardens and the Labyrinth and was made up of twelve stone pillars each the size of a carriage. The pillars glowed white from the 10,000 rains that had washed them. In the middle of the clearing was the ethereal imprint of a body that no amount of planting could cover over. "Some ancient evil must have happened there," Mr. Hawthorne told him once as they poured seed on the dead spot of the body's outline. "Been trying to get something to grow here since I was a lad little older than you and nothing ever takes."

The red moon shined upon the outline of the

body in the circle as Silas approached the stones. He had never stopped to tarry here after a day of work because Mr. Hawthorne said it wasn't safe to be near the gardens after dark. He touched one of the smooth stones and felt an odd thrumming through his body, as if great energy was stored inside them.

Arfast stepped from behind one of the stones. His wolf cloak was pulled tight over his head and its jaws dripped red in the light. "Let us prepare," he said with no humor in his face. "For tonight we journey to the land of death."

11
Deiva Enters the Clearing

They walked for so long that Lily wondered if they would ever see the outside world again. Cassandra was in front of her, holding a sputtering yellow candle that was little more than a nub. Lily followed, Abigail's journal tucked under one arm. Cobwebs hung like confetti from the ceiling of the secret passage. Occasionally, streams of light appeared on the walls, allowing them to peer into some rooms of the house. Cassandra made a rule against that as soon as they set out. "We'll only see things that frighten us," she said. "No matter how hard it is, we have to ignore whatever we hear." They'd done well so far. The crying, hooting, gibbering, and strange music coming from the other side of the walls only made them travel faster down the narrow corridor. Lily listened for the scuttling of spider legs on the stones behind them, but it was quiet. Still, when a cobweb tickled her neck, she had to bite down to keep from screaming out loud. When they came to an intersection where one secret passage met with another, they stopped to examine Abigail's map.

"We go this way," Cassandra said, pointing down the left-hand path. "We should get to Raga's and be back in plenty of time before we're missed."

"Do you think anyone else knows about these tunnels?" Lily asked as they set off again.

"From the dust on the floor, I'd say no. Nightfall Manor is impossible to know completely," Cassandra said. "It's like the Gardens that way."

"Don't you ever dream of leaving?" Lily asked.

"Where would I go? A green girl that — ," Cassandra cut herself off as she was about to say more. "No, the most I dream of is clearing the Gardens so Osbold, Father and I can live in peace."

"I don't mean to be rude — ," Lily said tentatively. She wanted to step lightly because she knew how easily Cassandra angered.

"But you're going to be. Go ahead," Cassandra said stopping.

"Why — why exactly are you green?" Lily asked and she cringed, waiting for Cassandra to explode at her.

The green girl tilted her head as if reflecting philosophically. "My mother was infected by an Angel Trumpet flower. What do you know about them?"

"Nothing," Lily said.

"Well, there's no reason you should. The only place they grow is in the shade of the Shadow Garden. Angel Trumpet is one of the most lovely and deadly plants. It has purple petals that hang like tentacles and white star-shaped flowers that can hypnotize a person if you stare too long at them."

"Hypnotize?" Lily said. They were walking along the musty passage again. The pounding and banging coming from under the house was growing distant now that they were going down a different tunnel.

"Angel Trumpet has a consciousness and thinks like a person, which makes it extra lethal. It's also incredibly patient. Angel Trumpet can wait for years to spring a trap. That was what happened with my mother. She passed the Shadow Garden every day on her way home and the Angel Trumpet watched and waited until its chance came. It hypnotized my mother into thinking there was gold in the high grass and when she went for it, the leaves grasped her, penetrating her skin until the stems wound their way to her heart."

"That's terrible," Lily said.

"By the time my father cut the vines loose, it was too late. She'd been poisoned and was dying. A week later, I was born… green. No one knows why, but my father swears it was because of the poison from the Angel Trumpet."

"I'm sorry," Lily said.

The passage was starting to smell of fresh earth.

A slight breeze stirred somewhere. The walls turned from stone to ancient mortar and then to dirt as they continued south.

"We're getting close," Cassandra said.

They came to the end of the passage as the candle sputtered to an end. Up ahead, light filtered through vines and a locked iron gate.

"So how do we get out of here?" Cassandra said pulling on the thick gate. "It'd take 20 men to open this."

"Let me have a look," Lily said. She pulled the gate and a lock clicked. The gate swung back, groaning on heavy hinges.

"How did you — ?" Cassandra looked irked that Lily had opened the door when she hadn't.

"I don't know," she said. *'I'm a Blackwood, that's how,'* Lily thought. *'It wouldn't work for anyone else, but it will always work for us.'*

Cassandra hacked at the vines with a knife that she kept in her belt and soon they pushed their way onto a trail behind the Shadow Garden.

Lily blinked in gray light. It had been more than three months since she'd been outside and her heart raced with her newfound freedom.

"I wish Silas could have met us here," she said.

"I've told you. It wouldn't be safe. Something's going on at the bunkhouse. Father's been down there a few times but he won't tell me what's happening. It's best if we do what we have to and get back. Your brother would only be a drag on us."

"You don't know Silas," Lily said. "He could help."

"The only way he could help is by staying out of our way," Cassandra said as they started down the path.

"I don't know what it is you have against him," Lily said.

"Really? You've never realized how insufferable he is, with that long mop of hair and those eyes that are different as night and day."

Lily laughed out loud, surprising herself at the sound. "So that's it, then?"

"What?" Cassandra asked.

"You like him. You like my brother," Lily teased.

"I do not. Why do you think that? Haven't I told you how much I hate him?"

"It's the way you say it," Lily said. She put her hands over her chest and faked a swoon. "Oh, his long hair and those dreamy eyes."

Cassandra's face contorted with rage and the green girl's cheeks reddened. "It's not true. Take it back. I can't stand him."

"Whatever you say," Lily said. "But you shouldn't be shy. It's just Silas. You'll have to bop him over the head if you want him to notice."

"I said I don't like him," Cassandra said through gritted teeth. She charged off ahead down the path and Lily had to run to catch up with her.

"I'm sorry," Lily said. "I'm only kidding."

"I don't want to talk about it anymore. I'm going

to get you to Raga and back inside and then I'm done. You Blackwoods can take care of yourselves."

Lily was about to respond when they heard the pounding of hooves coming toward them.

"Dusk riders," Cassandra said. "If they find us, they'll send you back to the house. Come on."

Before Lily could say anything, the green girl took off down the path. The impenetrable wall of the Labyrinth was to one side and open field stretching towards the mists to the other.

"Where are we going?" Lily said, gasping for breath.

"Don't worry, I know a place," Cassandra said. The horses racing towards them grew louder and Lily realized that they would be on them any second unless they found a place to hide. She looked to her left and stopped running. Her mouth dropped open. The path was empty. Cassandra had disappeared. "What the — ?"

"Over here," the green girl said, but all Lily saw was empty field with creeping mist that twisted and tumbled like curling smoke.

"Where?" Lily said. All she could see was the field, the mist, and the shadow of trees where the woods started.

"Here," Cassandra said, and her head appeared from nowhere.

Lily jumped back in surprise. "How did you do that?"

"No time. Get in here now!" Cassandra hissed.

Lily rushed toward her friend. For a second it felt like she was pushing through molasses, and then she was with Cassandra, looking out at the trail as the riders approached.

"What is this place?" she asked.

The green girl was crouched next to her, close enough that Lily could smell the earth and flower scent that radiated from her.

"Camouflage bush," she said. "They hide themselves out of defense. Try one of the berries and you'll see what I mean."

Brilliant red berries with white hairs grew in clusters on the rich green leaves of the bush. Lily plucked one and popped it in her mouth. Her tongue exploded with the taste of sugar, cream, and fresh strawberries. It was the best thing she'd ever eaten. She jammed the berries into her mouth as quickly as she could.

"So good," Lily said as red juice dribbled down her chin.

"No more," Cassandra said. "That's why the bush hides itself. Its berries, its leaves, everything about it is useful in one way or another. People aren't able to help themselves and they strip them bare until the plant dies."

Lily fought back an impulse to continue eating the berries and wiped her hands on the ground. Outside, the riders slowed. There were three men dressed in wolf cloaks. One of them was gargantuan. He barely fit on the poor horse whose legs buckled under his weight. The man had a big, pitted moon face and scraggily beard.

"If I were you, Larkspur, I would have taught One-Arm a lesson that he wouldn't forget," a rider said.

"All in good time," Larkspur said. He took a filthy knife from his belt and began picking his teeth. "Skuld will find his loyalty to Jonquil counts for nothing when Blackwood dies."

He spit out the last part of the sentence and the others laughed. "Things will be different. You'll see. We work too hard and for what? The evils are trapped. The gates are closed and still we ride around and around these grounds until our heads spin."

"What are you thinking, then?"

"Patience," Larkspur said. "Deiva will be dead soon, as will Jonquil. That leaves only the boy and his sister. Old Larkspur fancies himself head of the manor house with the Blackwood girl as his bride." The gelatinous dusk rider wetted his fingers with his lips and ran them through his greasy hair. "How could she resist me?"

The girls stayed hidden inside the bush until the last of the laughter faded, and then they crawled back out of the bush onto the path. Lily shuddered at the thought of what she'd heard.

"What did he mean about my uncle? Is something wrong with him?" she asked.

"I don't know," Cassandra said. "My father tells me little of what happens at their camp."

"And my brother?"

"Perhaps I'm not as cordial as I could be," the green girl said. Her cheeks reddened again. "I could talk with him."

"Please do," Lily said. "If what this man, Larkspur, said is true, then there are greater dangers here than I thought."

They hurried down the path into the mist until it felt as though they were walking through clouds. The fog hung in patches above the ground and the air was damp. The earth was wet and slick under their feet and moss grew along the sides of the giant trees. A path, barely big enough for one person, led further into the gloomy woods.

"Raga will expect a treat from us for the reading," Cassandra said as they lost sight of the field and were enveloped by the mist. "She has a sweet tooth."

"What are we going to give her?" Lily said. It was hard for her to believe some ancient witch would like cake and cookies.

Cassandra pulled out a handkerchief filled with berries from the camouflage bush. "Aren't you glad you have me as a friend?" she smiled.

They continued along the path until they were lost in a dreamscape of fog and darkness.

"Who is Raga? How'd she get here?" Lily asked shivering. Along with the mist that blocked the light, it was also much colder here than in the gardens.

"She came from New Salem, many years ago, when they burned anyone they thought to be a witch at the stake. One day, a little boy fell from a tree and broke his leg. Raga happened to be nearby and used her healing powers on him. When he told his father, the townspeople broke into her cabin and arrested her. They would have burned her as well, even though she was a healer, but Raga used her magic to escape and fled until she came to Nightfall Gardens."

Cassandra turned to look at Lily. "Just a bit of advice when you meet her. Don't act shocked."

"What do you mean?"

"Her head's on backwards," Cassandra said as if embarrassed.

"Her head's on backwards?" Lily repeated.

"It happened when she tried to cast a transmigration spell decades ago and she's never been able to fix it. She's really self-conscious about it. You'll see."

A toadstool-looking cottage appeared out of the haze. The roof was thick with ivy and the walls were curved and bloated. As they approached, the door opened and a teenage girl with red hair and milky skin exited, wrapping a blue coat about her. She saw the two girls approaching, gasped, and fled into the woods with the swiftness of a gazelle. Seconds later she was swallowed by the fog.

"Who was that?" Lily asked.

"One of the mist people," Cassandra said. "Probably from Mare's Tail — that's the closest village to Nightfall Gardens."

'She looked like my mother,' Lily thought as they

knocked on the front door.

"I told you, silly girl, put one drop in his ale and he won't be able to resist you," a voice croaked like a wheezing accordion from inside.

"Raga, it's Cassandra," the green girl said.

"Eh? Why didn't you say so, love? There's nasty wolves and other naughties lurking in the woods these days. Not safe. Not safe at all." The door cracked open and Lily stared into the most wart-laden face she'd ever seen. A milky caul covered one of the witch's eyes, which swam pale blue behind the film. Raga was hunched over with age as though she were collapsing in on herself. She used a gnarled piece of oak as a cane and banged it on the floor with each step as she crossed her chamber. As Cassandra had warned, the most disconcerting thing was that the old woman's head and neck were facing the wrong direction on her body. Raga looked at them from over her shoulder blades as her body walked away. Lily blinked and tried not to stare.

"Fungus tea?" Raga asked. Her hands were reaching for a kettle over the fireplace while her head faced them.

"No, thanks," Cassandra said.

"To what do I owe this great pleasure? It's not every day the Lady of the Manor visits my humble abode." Raga cackled through the broken stumps of her teeth.

"We come seeking help," Cassandra said.

"Of course you do. That's the only reason people

come here," Raga said sadly. "Before we get down to business, what kind of sweet treats did you bring your dear auntie?"

"Berries from the camouflage bush," Cassandra said.

Raga licked her lips and a chain of drool formed on her whiskered chin. "Oh, delicious. You'll have to tell me where that bush is sometime. You know they're my favorite. Now come and feed your dear auntie."

Cassandra looked at Lily with helplessness in her eyes. "You'll have to do it. It's not safe for me."

"Why?" Lily asked, shuddering at the drooling crone in front of her.

"I can't — . Please, just do it and I'll explain later," she said. Cassandra shoved the handkerchief into Lily's hands careful not to make contact with her.

Lily unfolded the handkerchief and the red berries glowed in the firelight.

"Oh goody, goody," Raga said. She stepped backwards towards Lily and gave the floorboards a bang with her walking stick. "You wouldn't believe how hard it is to feed yourself this way."

"Do you have a spoon?" Lily asked.

"What for?" Raga said suspiciously.

"To feed you the berries," she responded.

"What's wrong with your fingers?" Raga said.

"Nothing."

"Then don't be shy," the old crone said. "All your answers will come after I eat."

Lily tried not to think of the grunting and slurping sounds as she fed the witch the berries. Instead, she thought of Paris and a mysterious dark-haired boy who was the best actor (besides herself) of the stage and what life might be like if she ever escaped Nightfall Gardens. When she was finished, the ancient witch sat on a stool, so that while her face was looking straight at the girls, her hands were warming themselves at the fireplace behind her.

"My compliments to the chef," Raga wheezed. Her dry lips were red from the berry juice. "Now, what is it you seek?"

Lily pulled Abigail's diary from her satchel and showed it to the crone. Raga's good eye flickered and followed the pages as Lily turned them. "We're trying to figure out what kind of magic my aunt used to guard this book."

"Powerful magic. Powerful magic indeed," the witch's tongue darted out. "But one that you hold the key to."

"What do I have to do?" Lily asked.

Raga walked backwards to a table covered in books, an hourglass, the skeleton of a cat and other odds and ends. She looked through the items until she found what she was looking for and then walked backwards until she turned around and handed a yellow claw to Lily.

"Gorgan claw," Raga said. "There are only three of those on the market. You wouldn't believe what I had to trade for it."

"What's it for?"

"This book will only reveal its secrets to a Blackwood," the witch said. "In order for it to do that, you have to spill your blood on it."

"Blood?" Lily felt as though she were going to faint.

"Use the Gorgon claw when the red moon is at its highest. Cut your palm and hold it over the pages. All will be revealed then."

Cassandra was looking out the window at the fog covering the glass. "We should go soon, before it gets too dark, or we won't be able to find our way."

"Is there any thing else I need to know?" Lily asked.

Raga cackled. "There are many things you need to know. Darkness is coming to Nightfall Gardens. Even now, Eldritch is free and the walls of the Gardens grow weaker with each minute. Woe to the world if they should fall. What Prometheus has bound is coming undone. The last of days is upon us."

"That doesn't sound very uplifting," Cassandra said sarcastically.

"You'll joke no more when darkness fills the world," Raga said. Her one good eye narrowed. "Now go. You'll get no more from Raga today, except this." The crone looked straight at Lily. "Beware of those who wish you well. They mean no good."

"What does that mean?" Lily asked.

The witch teetered and cackled to herself. "Don't wait so long before you visit your dear auntie," the witch said to Cassandra. She turned away so that her backside could be warmed by the fire and they were left staring at her stringy gray hair.

The mist swirled thicker outside and the sky was murkier. They found their way to the covered passage near the Shadow Garden and followed the tunnel back to Nightfall Manor. No sooner had the bookshelf swung open and they tumbled into Lily's room than Polly entered.

"I've been looking all over for you, I have," Polly said excitedly. The maid's skin oozed extra white in the light and milky tears spilled down puffy cheeks. If the grub had eyebrows she would have raised them at the two disheveled girls in front of her. "I won't ask what you've been up to. There's no time." Her rubbery lips quivered and fresh tears squeezed from her blank eyes. She wiped her face with her uniform and the sleeve came away wet and glistening.

"What's wrong?" Lily asked. She'd never seen the housekeeper so distraught.

"It's your Grandmother Deiva. She's taken a turn for the worst and is asking for you," Polly said sobbing anew.

"I have to go," Lily said to Cassandra. "I'll talk with you tomorrow."

The walk to her grandmother's room was the longest of her life. Lily could tell by the way Polly was crying that her grandmother didn't have much longer to live. *'I barely know her,'* Lily thought, imagining what Deiva might have been like before her husband had disappeared into the mist and the gilirot ate her away. She shuddered at the heavy burden that would fall upon her shoulders as the last of the Blackwood women.

Deiva was in worse shape then Lily thought she would be. Her grandmother was propped up with pillows on a gigantic canopied bed with carved lion's feet. The black veil covered the last remnants of her ravaged face. Raspy, phlegm-filled breathing made the veil flutter. Her bony hands were clasped together on top of the blankets. The room was fetid with the smell of unwashed skin and rotting meat. It was the first time Lily had seen her grandmother away from the sitting room where she waited for her husband to return. Ozy poured water from a carafe into a glass. His jacket was off and she could see the remnants of the bandages hanging in strips from his mummified body. "You must drink this," he said to Deiva. "You're burning alive."

Her grandmother waved him away. "I don't want any. I don't see what good a glass of water is going to do in my journey to the other side."

"You mustn't talk that way," Ozy said, a plume of dust coming from his mouth.

"Why? If you knew how I feel, you wouldn't carry such pity in your eyes. It'll be a relief to leave this body. I'll be reunited with Charles once more. Now where's my granddaughter?"

Lily stepped forward. "Right here, grandmother."

"There you are. I'm sorry to tell you this, but soon your life will be more pain than pleasure. Now is the time to leave your childhood behind and resign yourself to life as mistress of Nightfall Gardens." Deiva was overtaken by a hacking cough that went on for so long Lily was surprised to hear her speak when it was finished. "Don't — have — much — time," her grandmother said. "Everyone out but my dear granddaughter." Deiva shook her hand in exasperation at the servants.

"We'll be right outside the door," Polly said.

"With your ear pressed against it, no doubt," Deiva sniped.

When the servants were gone, her grandmother gestured to the bed. "Come sit next to me. It's a tragedy my sons can't be with me at this time. Still, I'm no longer surprised by the nasty bag of tricks life has in store."

"I can call for Jonquil and my brother," Lily said, taking her hands. She expected them to be cold but they burned with the last moments of her grandmother's life.

"I won't be seeing my poor lovesick son today. He was poisoned by the Eldritch. It's only a matter of time until he follows me into the clearing," Deiva coughed again and it sounded as though her lungs were about to break loose from her body. "I wish I'd been able to see your father. Thomas was the sweet one. Tell him everything I did was to protect the family and keep the world from sliding into chaos."

Lily nodded at her. "I will."

"Steel yourself," her grandmother said. "Soon you'll be mistress of Nightfall Gardens. As the last female Blackwood, the Gardens will rise up to try to kill you. You must be on your guard at all times. I wish I'd been able to teach you more, but it's only in the final moments of my life that I see clearly once more."

Her grandmother pointed to a gold-inlaid jewelry box on a dresser on the other side of the room. "Bring that to me." Lily handed it to her grandmother, and Deiva opened the box and dug around until she found what she was looking for: a thin silver chain with a purple amethyst hanging from it.

"Come here," her grandmother said. With shaking hands, she clasped the chain around Lily's neck.

"What is it?" Lily asked.

"They say it belonged to Pandora herself and that it holds great power. I never found it more than an ugly purple stone, but perhaps you'll have more luck with it."

Her grandmother coughed again so loudly that Lily was surprised when Deiva drew another breath and continued. "Now call Polly and Ozy back, they've been faithful servants through many dark times."

The door opened as if the two had been waiting to enter. Polly slid across the floor, leaving snail tracks in her wake, while Ozy staggered woodenly with his arms in front of him. His bandages hung in shreds from his arms.

"Oh, don't talk that way. You mustn't talk that way, my lady. You'll be fit as a bogrum in no time." The maid threw her arms around Deiva and they squelched against her.

"Now is not the time for lies, Polly. If one is ever to be truthful, it should be at the moment that they stare into the abyss. I'll be fine, love. I need you and Ozy to promise me one thing."

"Name it and it shall be done," Ozy said through a dusty cloud.

"Take care of my grandchildren as if they were your own," she said.

The mummy and snail nodded their heads. Tears grooved the parchment of Ozy's face and oozed down Polly's cheeks.

As the end of night approached in Nightfall Gardens, Deiva slipped away for good. The blood red moon was filtering through the windows when Deiva sat up and gave a great cry. Her veil slid off for an instant and Lily saw the grisly remains of her grandmother's face. She called out in great pain. "Charles! I see you! I'm coming!" With that, she flung herself back violently on the bed and was dead.

"She's gone, my lady is gone," Polly wailed, covering her face with her hands.

All was quiet and then a thrum started deep within the floors and walls of the house. The vibrating grew in power until it felt as if all of Nightfall Manor was coming undone. A shrieking came from everywhere at once, growing louder and louder until Lily jammed her hands over her ears to block the sound that threatened to burst her eardrums. Cracks formed in the walls and in the ceiling.

Hunks of plaster smashed to the floor. Lily grabbed a table to keep from losing her balance, while Polly suctioned herself to the floor. Ozy reached for a chair but lost his footing and fell; his body broke in two as it struck the ground. A great cloud of dust and dozens of tiny sparrows came out of his insides and circled the room. Deiva's bed rose three feet off the floor and smashed down, breaking the frame and tossing Deiva's body in the air like a rag doll. Then, as quickly as it had begun, the house stopped shaking and the noise quieted.

Lily stood on shaky feet, waiting for the noise that might start again at any second. "What was *that*?" She asked.

Polly kneeled in front of her and Ozy pulled his top half up so that he was facing Lily. "The house was telling us that the old Mistress has died and a new has taken her place. All hail the new queen of Nightfall Manor."

"All hail," Ozy said. The mummy grabbed for his legs, which were crawling away across the floor.

Lily felt embarrassed at how the servants were looking at her. "I'm no queen," she said through reddened cheeks.

"You don't have much say in the matter," Polly said, sniffling. "There's no time to mourn your grandmother like we should. There are too many preparations to make."

"Preparations?" Lily asked.

"We must prepare the feast for the gathering," Polly said.

"What gathering?" Lily asked.

"Oh dear, she doesn't know," Ozy said. He had caught his legs and was attempting to wrap his midriff back together with bandages.

The maid wiped the tears from her face and straightened her uniform. Her bald head gleamed like an exposed grub under a rock in the morning light. "Whenever a head of the house dies, a momentary truce is called and one representative from each of the Gardens is allowed into the house to pay tribute to the deceased."

"Those things — are coming here?" Lily said incredulously.

"*One* representative from each of the Gardens. They are honor-bound to do no ill while inside. When the feast is finished, your grandmother's body will be taken outside and burned on a pyre. It's a tradition that goes back to the founding of this place."

'Emissaries from the gardens are coming. Why do I fear this doesn't bode well,' Lily thought. She looked once more at the lifeless body of Deiva and covered her mutilated face with the veil. She walked to the

window and looked out at the rain-sopped grounds. Her reflection stared back at her in the glass and the amethyst necklace, the one Pandora had worn, mocked her. Her first day dawned as the new head of Nightfall Gardens.

12
Inside the White Garden

"Smear yourself with this," Arfast said. "And be quick. It's not safe to linger so near the Gardens after dark."

The rider handed Silas a canvas bag filled with a foul-smelling green manure that writhed with juicy worms and glowed green in the gray of night. Silas took one whiff of the contents of the sack and felt as if he was going to vomit. "What is it?" he gagged.

"Manticore excrement," Arfast said. "But it's not that we're interested in. The bettlebaum maggot that grows inside of it contains a special property that, when smeared on a person, makes them appear as whoever the viewer wants them to be. We'll sneak in, get the Fairy Bells and be out before anyone's the wiser."

"If it's that easy, why didn't we do it before?"

Silas asked.

"Because the bettlebaum loses its power an hour or two after application. So we have to hurry. That is, unless you fancy spending eternity in the White Garden," Arfast said. His eyebrows looked devilish in the glow coming from the worms.

"No thanks," Silas said. He took a huge gulp of fresh air and reached his hand into the bag and tried not to think about the worms wriggling in his fingers. When his hand was full, he smeared it on his face and neck. He held his breath until he thought his lungs might burst and then gasped in the burning stench of manticore poop.

"This — is — too — much," Silas said, rubbing it through his hair and reaching in to the bag for another handful.

Arfast laughed. "It's not so bad, especially if you have daisy dollops in your nose." The rider tilted his head so Silas could see the yellow plugs that were stuffed up his nostrils.

"What do they do?"

"Make everything smell fresh as a daisy," Arfast said. The grin spread wider on his face.

"I don't suppose you could have gotten some for me as well," Silas said irked.

"And deprive you of this once-in-a-lifetime experience? I don't think so," the rider smiled.

"Gee, thanks," Silas said. He rubbed himself vigorously with the contents of the sack and tried to ignore Arfast, who whistled while he covered himself with beetlebaum juice as if he were bathing in a fresh mountain spring.

When he had finished, Silas was surprised to find that he glowed green like the maggots. Arfast rubbed the last of the bag through his hair and he too, was lit with a strange luminescence. The rider brushed off a maggot that was crawling on his cheek. "All right, let's go. Just follow me and we'll be as quick as silver."

The entrance to the White Garden was close; they were there in minutes. Red moonlight spilled on the empty promenade, washing it the color of blood. The hooded ancient statue was cloaked in shadows.

"Keep quiet and don't talk unless spoken to," Arfast whispered. "These things have been dead for a long time and many of them are insane. They're easy enough to fool as long as you don't overdo it. Stay close."

With that, Arfast stepped on the pathway that led along the promenade. Silas looked back toward Nightfall Manor and wondered what his sister was doing at that moment. *'I hope you're safer than me,'* he thought, then followed Arfast into the White Garden.

Nothing changed. The same red moon shone overhead. The same breeze tickled his neck and cooled his skin. Nothing lunged from the woods to attack them. Only when he looked down did he receive his first shock. The walkway crunched under his boots. The sound was abnormally loud and reminded him of stepping on seashells at the beach. *'What stone is this?'* he thought, nudging a flake free from the walk. A finger bone poked up from the earth. Nearby, several pairs of rib bones made up the path. How could he have been so blind? Thousands of human bones formed the walk as well as the benches under the trees.

Arfast slowed when he realized Silas wasn't following him. "I know," he said. "But we must keep moving, unless you want to end up part of the scenery."

Silas closed his eyes and hurried after the rider. Seen from the other side, the ancient begrimed statue was clearly the grim reaper, a skeleton face hooded in robes swinging a scythe through stalks of wheat, the strands of which were ornately carved miniatures of human beings. As he watched, Silas saw the figures dance, twisting in torment. Images came into his mind: a homeless man was stabbed to death on a street in New Amsterdam, a flood wiped out a village in Asia, and an earthquake killed thousands in South America. Each moment, one person died and another was born; the cycle repeated itself, over and over. The reaper came for everyone, guiding them along the path to a new beginning. Silas pulled his eyes away. Whatever lived in the White Garden perverted this. Death was the natural order of life, but the creatures here fed off people's fear of their earthly end. It was the fear that gave them power. He cast one last glance back and followed Arfast.

They came to another part of the garden. Steps of crunching bone led down to a tangled mass of grapevines full of cherry-colored grapes so ripe that they looked as though they would burst at the first bite. Another path split off into an overhang of trees. It was along this path that Silas and Arfast saw a brilliant yellow light bobbing towards them.

"Into the vineyard," Arfast said. He shoved Silas into the grapevines and they weaved their way among the vines.

Silas's hands trembled as the beast appeared in the bloody moonlight. He'd never seen anything like it before in his life and hoped he'd never see something so horrible again. The monster had a piggish snout with waxen yellow skin and coarse, bristly hair sprouting in wisps from its head. Its eyes looked as though they'd been dipped in black ink. The creature snorted and grunted as he walked. It wore tattered robes and was holding a lantern in one hoof-like hand that was lit by a pair of sprites. Silas caught a glimpse of them as the creature passed; the sprites weren't much longer than his index finger and they radiated a powerful light, though one's glow was much weaker than the other's. The one with the lesser light collapsed at that moment and his light blinked out before fizzling back into existence. The other sprite rushed to his friend, but the horror holding the lantern shook it with impatience. The sprites were flung from one side of the glass to the other.

"Oh no, you don't," the pig-like creature

snorted. "You can rest when you're dead. I didn't trade good human meat for a bunch of layabouts."

"You're killing us," the stronger sprite said in an insect buzz.

"You just now noticed that, eh? It only took you a decade to figure that out? Smart as a whip, you fairies," the creature grunted with laughter. "This is the garden of death, don't you understand that? You'd have been better off staying in the Shadow Garden where you lot belong. Now shut up and light the way or I'll shake this jar until you turn to jam."

The stronger sprite dragged his friend to his feet and his light flickered a little more powerfully, illuminating the long whiskers growing out of the beast's cheeks. "That's better," the pig creature said continuing down the path until the light disappeared into the trees.

"What was that?" Silas whispered as they rose to their feet.

"A Jinkinki," Arfast said. "Malevolent creatures with a taste for the flesh of people who've died. To feed that, they live in cemeteries and other dark places. Once they become fixated on one of the living, obsession overtakes them and they'll do anything to feast on that person's remains. They'll follow their prey to the gates of Hell and can even appear in their dreams."

"They sound lovely," Silas gulped.

"Oh, there's much worse here," Arfast said. "Now come along. We don't have much time."

Silas followed Arfast along the path the Jinkinki had just come from until they were deep in the shadows of the walk. Strange plants wrapped around the trees. The crimson moonlight flickered off of a pond up ahead.

"I hope you know where you're going," Silas said after they'd been walking for a while. "How many times have you been here?"

"Zero. This is my first time," Arfast whispered.

"What?" Silas stopped. "I thought you knew where the Fairy Bells grew."

"I've seen the maps drawn by the other riders. Sometimes there's a need to spy what's happening in the gardens. Each time, the maps are fleshed out a little more."

"The gardens aren't that big," Silas said, thinking how he'd just walked around the White Garden with Mr. Hawthorne earlier that day.

"From the outside," Arfast said. He started walking again. "From the inside, distances are funny. I've heard you could walk for days and not see all of what's inside here. Now, off we go."

As they approached the still pond, Silas heard the most ear-splitting shriek of his life coming from the direction of the house. The noise was so terrible that he thrust his hands over his ears out of fear his eardrums would burst. The ground shook under his feet and for a moment, he thought the earth was going to open and swallow him whole. The sound stopped as quickly as it began. Then, in unison, all the windows in Nightfall Manor lit up and he could clearly make out Arfast with the dripping manticore dung coating his face and the mossy water of the pond as well as the minutest details of the leaves around him. There was silence for a second and then a cheer burst from all of the Gardens at once: a combination of roars, snarls, screams, screeches, squeals, howls, yowls, gibbering, babbling and hissing. The woods came alive at once and, if Arfast hadn't thrown him to the side right then, they would probably have both died. Out of the trees shot a shrouded figure traveling at a speed that would have pulverized them if they had collided. The apparition sped past and its mere presence was so foul that Silas felt physically ill at its proximity. The apparition dove into the water and disappeared, sending a spray of water twenty feet into the air. It was gone for several seconds and then burst back out from under the water and shot into the air, spinning in a circle and shrieking with the sound of rusty nails dragging across a sheet of tin. The ghost shot off like a bullet and was away over the trees so quickly Silas pinched himself to make sure that what had happened was real. The Gardens were restless with the sounds that came from them.

"What's happening?" Silas asked.

"I don't know," Arfast said. "But it can't be good, the way they are celebrating."

They hurried along the trail, catching glimpses of spirits and other monstrosities that lived inside of the garden. They ran onto a great lawn where dozens of silent black figures stood in circles, forms without features. They were darker than the night, darker than anything Silas had ever seen. They were the absence of light personified.

Silas almost ran into one of the figures, but Arfast grabbed him and they slowly weaved their way through the silent figures until they were on the other side of the lawn.

"Shades," Arfast whispered to him, once they were running again.

Up ahead, a bridge passed over an archway. On the other side was an abandoned fountain.

"Getting closer," Arfast said. "I remember this from the map."

They plunged ahead, bones crunching underfoot. *'How much time do we have?'* Silas wondered. *'20 minutes? 30 minutes?'* When they passed under the bridge, they were enveloped in darkness. Silas saw yellow eyes following him and Arfast through the tunnel, then they were out the other side and in the middle of the most raucous party he'd ever seen. Most of the inhabitants of the White Garden were there. The promenade around the fountain was filled with thousands of death's minions and those that clung to death like barnacles on a ship. There were ghosts and shades, banshees and ghouls that plucked bodies straight from the crypt. Silas saw creatures with tentacles and fangs and apparitions that froze him to his core. Something that looked like a gigantic cockroach with a human face and bisected eyes droned words that were vaguely human.

"She's dead. She's dead. The walls grow weaker," the cockroach said brushing against him.

He saw goat-headed creatures with pentagrams and a white worm the length of the bunkhouse that pushed its way up through the ground, its red mouth open as it sucked in air for the first time in a century.

Horrors. There were so many of them that Silas closed his eyes to block them out lest he go insane. Even Arfast seemed terrified of the countless creatures and mad exultation that was taking place. Among the residents of the White Garden walked the Lords of Death, with long withered faces and purple skin who were old when the world was new. They tottered amongst the crowd on walking sticks made from Joshua Trees and were so repellent that even the succubi and minor deities cleared a path for them.

"We have to go," Arfast said, circling the crowd, making sure to stay as far from the monstrosities as he could.

Silas followed, holding his breath, certain that at any moment the bettlebaum would wear off and he would be visible to all of the creatures, just long enough for them to fall on him and feast on his bones. No one seemed to notice them though, and they pushed through the crowd and made their way around the fountain.

"What's put a penny in their pocket?" Silas asked as they headed away from the celebration.

"Whatever it is doesn't bode well," Arfast said. "Few things in the Gardens do though."

Silas was thinking on this when a shade leaped on the fountain and transformed into his grandmother before his eyes. One moment, the shade was long as a shadow on a hot summer day and the next it was Deiva in her black dress and veil. His grandmother pulled up her skirt and began high kicking on the fountain as the creatures erupted with maniacal laughter.

"Look away," Arfast said, attempting to shield Silas, but the boy dodged away from him.

When she was finished dancing, his grandmother fell into the crowd and was carried on the shoulders of a cross between a giant and a mole. The creature was covered in putrid gray fur, with no eyes and shovel-like claws for hands. The mole giant bellowed and cleared a path in front of him with each step he took. Deiva was lofted high above the crowd before eventually turning back into the shade and swan diving into the mob.

"Now only the girl holds us here," a demon near them said. The demon swirled a mixture of red and black. Horns jutted from his forehead. His eyes were rivers of fire. "And she won't be alive for long."

He would have listened to more, but Arfast jerked hard on his arm. "Come along. Now!"

"My grandmother's dead," Silas said sorrowfully when they were far from the jubilant crowd and the calm night of the garden surrounded them once again.

"I'm sorry to hear that. There'll be time enough for mourning when we're out of here," Arfast said. He stopped at a crossroads and scratched his head, trying to figure out which direction they should go.

"I didn't even know I had a grandmother until Jonquil kidnapped my sister," Silas said. "I only met her one time."

"Sometimes that makes it all the worse," Arfast said, making a decision and turning them down one of the paths.

They walked up a hill toward a cave with an opening wide enough for a dozen people to walk through.

"We're here," Arfast whispered in his ear. "Cerberus's home. The Fairy Bells grow near here. Look for something that glows white. Be quick about it, in case he comes back."

Silas waded through the undergrowth near the rocks looking for the white flowers. He felt as if his every step made enough noise to wake the whole garden. Even from here, the faint sounds of celebration could be heard. Something gleamed in the moonlight, but when he bent to examine it, a toadstool burst and oozed yellow pus at his touch. Arfast was on the other side of the clearing and was having as little success as he was. Silas worked his way closer to the cave. Cold air rushed out of the opening and he smelled animal droppings and the ripe smell of an un-bathed dog. This was Cerberus's lair, where the three-headed monstrosity lived. He was the old guardian of Hades, whose job was to ensure the dead didn't escape back to the land of the living. Now he was trapped here, along with the rest of the emissaries who used the name of death to torment human kind.

"Did you find it yet?" Arfast said. His hands were empty and he looked worried. "It has to be around here somewhere. Maybe further in the woods. I swore that the other riders told me the Fairy Bells grew in Cerberus's… " Arfast trailed off and glanced into the cave. Something flashed white from the inside.

"Wait here," Arfast said, about to enter.

"Let me look," Silas said. "I'm smaller, plus you can keep a look out for pug ugly in case he comes back."

"Be quick, then," Arfast said, climbing onto one of the rocks so he could see anything that might approach.

A pungent animal aroma filled his nostrils, becoming stronger with every step Silas took into the cave. Bones were scattered about the den, but whether they were human or otherwise, he couldn't tell. Water dripped from far back in the recesses. He moved deeper inside toward the luminescence that existed like the only light in the universe. The entryway was no bigger than a stamp behind him. Silas was close enough that he could make out the dazzling array of hundreds of delicate flowers growing from the walls. Tiny red veins ran through the translucent petals. They trembled as he plucked them and stuffed them in his bag.

He was standing to leave when he heard the forlorn singing of a nightingale coming from outside the cave. Cerberus was coming back! Silas hurried toward the entry in time to see the lumbering beast making its way toward him. The monstrosity was only a dog by the loosest definition of the term. It stood as high as a house and was wide enough that it must have been a snug fit for him in the cave. Cerberus's legs were as thick as oak trees, with nails that were as long as railroad spikes. Most terrifying of all were the three heads on his shoulders, which were in constant argument with each other. The heads were wider and flatter than a regular dog's and they moved with fluidity, biting, snapping, and growling at each other with such intensity that Silas was surprised they were able to tell where they were going. The hound of Hades shook the ground as he approached.

Silas edged out of the cave as Cerberus reached the entrance. The monster raised one of its heads and sniffed the air; its nose recoiled as though it scented something foul on the wind. Silas felt as if his heart was about to pound free of its ribcage. The monster sniffed inside the cave and then turned one of its heads and began smelling near where Silas was hidden. From this close he could make out the yellow eyes of the creature and see it was covered in a black fur no thicker than a seal's coat. There was a reason it was the hellhound's job to make sure no one escaped from the underworld. Silas didn't want to imagine what it would feel like to have the beast fall upon him, rending him to shreds. Even centuries in the White Garden hadn't dulled its senses. Cerberus sniffed closer and closer to where Silas was. The boy pressed himself against the rocks, willing himself to disappear into them if possible. Its nose was inches from his face, and a white froth dripped from jaws that looked powerful enough to pull his head from his shoulders with one bite. Silas held his breath, afraid the slightest exhalation would reveal his presence. From above, rocks slid down and bounced around him. One of them struck Cerberus on his middle head. In anger, it turned and snapped at the head smelling for Silas. Suddenly, all three heads were biting and tearing at each other, trying to catch each other by the throat. While Cerberus was fighting himself, Silas slid down the wall and ran back up the path, the sound of the dog's growling and snapping fading behind him. Minutes later, Arfast caught up with him.

"How'd you manage that?" Silas asked.

"They must get on each other's nerves something terrible after so many millennia together," Arfast said grinning. "Imagine not even being able to change your underwear in private."

The two raced down the path. The moon, a malignant red eye, followed them overhead. They skirted the fountain where the celebration was as lively as ever. Shrouded figures glided on the air above the crowd, the same color and consistency as smoke. One of the figures strummed a guitar made of human hair and bones. The crowd was gathered in some hellish sing-along that sounded like every chalkboard in the world was being scraped at exactly the same time. Silas pressed his fingers over his ears and kept running.

The next few minutes were a blur as they switched from one path to another, trees and plants closing in from all sides. Silas felt a burning stitch in his side. Ahead, he caught a glimpse of the entrance to the White Garden. Arfast swerved from the trail and cut through the trees in that direction. "Shortcut!" he laughed. Silas chased him, trying to hold back the whoop in his own heart and that was how he ran into the Jinkinki.

One moment he was plunging through the trees and the next his feet were flying out from under him. Silas tumbled through the air and came down hard on the ground. He rolled on his side, clutching the bag to make sure he hadn't lost the precious Fairy Bells. Something stirred on the earth near him. Piggish eyes blinked from muck, next came a snout, followed by a head and face. Silas gasped and jumped to his feet. It was the Jinkinki that they had encountered earlier in the night. This must be his den. He was buried in the ground, but as Silas watched, the creature began dragging itself out of the earth.

"Flesh, I smell sweet flesh," the Jinkinki slathered. "Oh, it's been so long. So very long."

The piggish creature flopped and crawled its way out of the pit toward him. Silas was going to run for it when a blinding light flashed on in the tree next to him. Silas threw his hands over his eyes to shield them. It was the sprites. The lantern that they were trapped in was hanging from a nearby branch.

"Boy, set us free," the stronger sprite said in an insect buzz. The sprite was an outline of pure gold light with wings and nothing more. "He's killing my friend."

At that moment, the Jinkinki lunged at Silas, grabbing for his ankle. The creature was halfway out of the earth now. "Oh sweet, tender, juicy, succulent human flesh, how long I've waited for thee." The Jinkinki re-doubled his efforts to free himself.

"Smash the lantern, please," the sprite said. "We'll help you escape."

'Never trust anything that lives in the gardens,' Mr. Hawthorne told him, one afternoon as they cleared the trails. 'They'll turn on you the moment they get the chance.' Silas looked into the cage and saw how weak the glow was emanating from the other sprite. It was leaning against the side of the lantern glass as though it didn't have the strength to stand. Silas made up his mind in that instant and grabbed the lantern from the branch.

"No, wait! What are you doing?" The Jinkinki

oinked.

Before the monster could say another word, Silas smashed the lantern against the tree, shattering the glass into a thousand shards. Both of the sprites raced and zipped through the air with their newfound freedom.

"I'll roast you on a spit for that, boy," the Jinkinki said, kicking the last of the dirt off as he pulled himself free with one final shake.

Silas could wait no longer. He bounded through the bushes and trees into the clearing, and back to the promenade. Up ahead, Arfast was running toward him. The dusk rider had finally realized the boy was missing. The sprites danced around his ears, shooting one way and then the other.

"Thank you, boy. He trapped us decades ago and has made us do his evil will since then. He would have killed us if we'd been there much longer. We're indebted to you now. If you ever need us, just say our names, Ulfeid and Tofa, and we'll come." With those words, the sprites zipped away, pinpricks of light that disappeared in the night sky.

Behind him, Silas heard a squeal of anger. He turned to see the Jinkinki against the dark outline of the trees.

"A Jinkinki never forgets a wrong," the creature squealed at him. "I'll find you one of these days, boy, and I'll strip your flesh from you before I feast on your innards. Mark my words. This isn't the last you've seen of me. You'll pay dearly for crossing me."

It wasn't until the two had passed safely out of the White Garden that Arfast asked what happened.

"Getting up to some mischief, I see," the dusk rider said. "I'd be on your guard though. You've made a mortal enemy out of that Jinkinki. They fret and obsess over every slight done to them and won't stop until they've gotten their blood vengeance."

"But he's trapped in the Garden," Silas said as they walked to the bunkhouse.

"The walls that bind them are growing weaker. Best be prepared: Jinkinki's never forget. They will hound their prey a lifetime and chase them to the furthest corners of the world to seek vengeance."

The bunkhouse was deserted when they arrived except for Ezekiel, the camp cook. The rest of the riders were on patrol, making sure that nothing was escaping from the gardens as they celebrated Deiva's death. Even from inside the bunkhouse, Silas heard the terrifying howling and bellowing coming from outside. It was a restless sound, the sound of something that had been trapped for a long, long time but was finally close to being free.

"I tell you I never heard anything like it," old Ezekiel said. He was frail and enfeebled and hadn't ridden in years. Now he served as cook, a task that he was ill suited for but that he'd been relegated to in his twilight years. Ezekiel was balding with stringy gray hair that fell from his sides to his shoulders. "In all my years, I never heard the gardens so... so alive, sounding like everything was going to spill out at once."

"Let's hope for our sakes it doesn't, old man," Arfast said. "Otherwise, no amount of riders will hold back what's inside."

Arfast and Silas went to Jonquil who looked closer to death than ever. His face was the same color as the sheets on his bed. When Silas touched his forehead it was ice cold and only the faintest pulse throbbed in his neck.

"He'll be in the shadowland before too long," Ezekiel said. "Shame, too. I always liked Jonquil. He was a proper leader, not like that bloated windbag Larkspur who's apt to take his place."

"That may not happen if we act quickly," Arfast said. "Silas, fetch some hot water and rags. Zeke, I need the pestle and mortar you use to grind your herbs."

Silas heated the water over the fire as Arfast ground the Fairy Bells into powder.

"Are those what I think they are?" Ezekiel said. His eyes grew wide as Arfast poured the last of the flowers into the mortar and began grinding them.

"Aye," Arfast said. "Straight from the White Garden itself."

"I might have to start re-evaluating my opinion of you, lad," Ezekiel said chuckling.

"As long as I don't have to re-evaluate my opinion of your cooking," Arfast said.

Silas brought the hot water over to Arfast, who

let it cool for a minute before pouring the powder and water into a cup.

"If anything can stop Eldritch's poison, it's this," Arfast said. "Go ahead and give it to him, boy."

Silas took a deep breath and parted his uncle's dry lips. He tilted Jonquil's head and poured the steaming liquid down his throat, slowly at first. *'Come on, wake up,'* he thought. The cup was almost empty now. He gave the last of it to Jonquil.

The three of them sat and waited. Minutes passed. Outside, the sounds in the Gardens continued as loud as ever. The candle burned lower on the table. Ezekiel was the first to stand. "Well lads, it was worth a try," he said.

At that moment, Jonquil stirred. Silas bent closer and saw the color was flushing back to his cheeks. He touched Jonquil's skin and felt his temperature returning to normal.

"I think its working," Silas said.

As if he'd heard, Jonquil opened his eyes and stared straight at them. In a ragged voice, he asked. "Where am I?"

13
The Emissaries

Lily finished clasping the amethyst necklace that had belonged to Deiva and all of the other Blackwood women going back to Pandora and examined herself in the bedroom mirror. What she saw would have made most girls her age (as well as adults) flee in terror. Maggots writhed in the decomposing flesh of her face and hands. Pieces of skin rotted away on her cheeks. Two holes stared from where her nose should have been and her upper lip was stripped away to reveal exposed teeth. "It's a projection mirror, my lady," Ursula told her one morning as she dusted and sang a song about rain clouds. "Thrives off fear. Can't hurt you none, though." Once she realized that, Lily began to use the mirror, just to show she *wasn't* afraid. What the mirror couldn't distort was the beautiful green dress made especially for this occasion, the shimmering purple necklace that she wore or the fact that her white blond hair was pinned to the sides and fell in curls around her face. She straightened her dress and turned the mirror around. Her guests should have arrived by now and there was no way she could avoid them any longer. It was time for her to meet the emissaries from the three gardens.

"Polly," she called and the door opened almost immediately.

"Yes, my lady," the housemaid said. Even the gigantic slug looked as though she'd spruced up for the event. Her skin glistened with an extra milky white sheen and her maid's uniform was newly washed.

"Are my guests here?" Lily asked.

"They are waiting in the dining room for you, just now, miss."

"Well, let's not keep them waiting longer," Lily said, a slight tremble to her voice. She didn't know what to expect. She hadn't been close to any of the beings living in the gardens, other than her glimpses into the Shadow Garden from the upstairs windows. Lily thought of the executioner beheading her in the macabre play that had been put on for her. *'Everything in the Gardens wants me dead,'* Lily thought shuddering. *'I must remember that.'*

As if Polly could read her mind, the housemaid said "Don't be a-scared, my lady. This pact was made longer ago than you or I can comprehend. A promise was made that on this night, the evil here can do no harm. The house would turn against them if they tried anything."

Lily nodded and followed the maid down to the dining room. She heard chairs scraping, silverware clattering and voices whispering as she entered the stadium-sized room. Three figures were sitting at the mammoth table intensely immersed in conversation. Ozy poured red wine into crystal glasses. The mummy seemed to have recovered from being broken in half. The telltale signs of wrapping were hanging from his jacket sleeves and he moved at his usual glacially slow shuffle. Lily couldn't take her eyes off the three figures that bowed as she approached the table. She had expected the representatives to be monsters and look anything but human: two of the three, though, could have passed for people — very ill people, but humanoid nonetheless. The third's top half was human and the bottom was reptilian. Scales glittered in the candlelight and Lily saw the swish of a tail under the table.

As Lily approached, her heart leapt into her throat. She was so nervous that she was frightened her legs might buckle. Cold rushed to greet her the closer she came to them, until frost exhaled from her mouth in wisps. The first who rose to greet her was a teenage boy who couldn't have been much older than she was. He bowed and reached for her hand. Lily had never seen anyone like him before. His hair was obsidian black, and sad sea-green eyes rode above his chiseled cheekbones. There was a pallor about him that bespoke sickness and days spent indoors. The boy's lips formed a pout as she yanked her hand back. Lily had already decided that none of them were going to touch her, even if it was rude. The air grew colder around her.

"Francois Villon," the boy said and there was the slightest foreign accent to his words. He smiled and displayed a mouthful of perfect teeth. "I come from the White Garden. No one mentioned how beautiful you are."

Lily felt her face flush. She was used to being complimented, but she wasn't used to it coming from someone as good-looking as the boy blocking her way. *'French,'* she thought. *'I've never heard it spoken before but I've always imagined that's what it must sound like.'* She stared into the fathom of his eyes.

"Thank you. You're too gracious," she said, bowing back at him.

"Merci, madam of Nightfall Gardens. I'm sorry to hear about the loss of your grandmother. She was a tenacious opponent." He moved aside so she could greet her other guests.

"She was at that," the second guest said. The woman standing in front of Villon was so pale she made him look as if he'd just come back from a holiday in the tropics. Alabaster was the only word to describe how absolutely white and bloodless her skin was. There wasn't a touch of pigment upon her anywhere; even her gray eyes were leeched of their original color. Her raven hair fell to the small of her back and her shoulder bones jutted from the emaciated flesh of her frame. She was tall, taller than Silas, taller than Jonquil, and so thin she listed as if about to blow over in the wind. The almost smile ratcheted on her face resembled the painting of the Mona Lisa that Lily had seen once in a book. The puzzling smile never left her face. There was something eerie about the fact that no matter what was said, no matter how sad or disturbing, the grin never left her. It fell on Lily like a hammer blow that this was one of the "Smiling Ladies," the three women she'd seen walking in the Shadow Garden. She remembered Ursula's terrified reaction to them. "It's the Smiling Ladies, miss. Oh, terrible. Pray you never come face to face with them. Oh, pray, miss," Ursula had said. Lily had to hold back from rubbing her arms to stave off the cold.

"I see by your face you recognize me," the woman said. "My name's Esmeret. I'm one of three sisters from the Shadow Garden. You must come and visit us sometime. It would be a real — treat." Her mouth opened far enough that Lily glimpsed a pair of gigantic pearl-colored fangs before Esmeret's lips closed over them.

Lily nodded. The last place she would ever willingly go was into the Gardens. She could only imagine what would await her there.

The last guest slithered out from behind the dining table. The top half of the creature was woman while the bottom half was snake. Her tail was covered in multifaceted scales and ended in a rattle that shook with the sound of beads rolling inside a crackly paper bag. A forked tongue flicked out of her mouth and her body moved with slithering gyrations.

"Noooooooooo. You muuuuuusssst come to the Labyrinth. That's where you belong, your grace," the snake-woman said, her eyes flashing yellow and green. "There are wonders there that human eyes have not sssssssseeeeeeennnn in many yearssss." The snake-woman came to a stop in front of her. The room grew abnormally quiet. Even the laughter and banging pots from the kitchen could not be heard. Lily saw Polly wringing her mucous hands. Ozy seemed extra alert, though what good they could do was doubtful. *I must have faith the house will protect me,'* Lily thought. *'I can't back down, because that's what they want. They want me to be scared.'*

"I'm afraid you'll have to tell me all about them at dinner, as I won't be able to visit the Labyrinth or any of the Gardens for the foreseeable future," Lily said.

The snake-woman lowered her head. "As you wish. Sometimes trips do arise unexpectedly. You never know where you might end up one day."

"Oh, quit with the theatrics, Kadru," Francois Villon said, rolling his eyes. "This is our first time out of the Gardens in half a century and you want to waste it on veiled threats. I'd rather have good wine and conversation before being sent back to that abysmal hole."

"Yooooooouuu would," Kadru, the snake-woman said. "That's why the White Garden hassss fallen into sssssuch sssssad dissssrepair in recent yearssss."

"Please," Villon said, scoffing. "If the White Garden had been collapsing as long as you suggest it would be a vegetable patch by now." The Frenchman grabbed a bottle of wine from the table and poured himself a large glass. "Enough of this fighting and dissention. We're here to pay our respects to a worthy adversary, Deiva. We may have been on different sides, but she was smart enough never to walk into one of the traps we set for her." With that, he tossed back the glass of wine and sighed. "Fa fait longtemps," he muttered to himself.

Kadru's rattle grew louder until it filled the room. The snake-woman's eyes narrowed and for a moment it seemed as though she might attack Villon, but then the rattle quieted and she slithered back to her seat.

"You'll have to forgive my friends. They aren't used to being in polite company," Esmeret said. Her voice was an icy purr.

"Speak for yourself," Villon said, pouring another glass of wine. "There was a time when everyone knew me."

"That helped you no more than it did the rest of uuusssss," Kadru hissed.

The three bickered as Lily took a seat at the head

of the table. What had Villon meant by saying Deiva had escaped every trap set for her? There was so much for her to learn. Who would teach her now that her grandmother was gone? Lily had never noticed such darkness in the dining room before. Not even the candles along the walls illuminated the black pitch that settled in the corners. As she stared, she thought she saw a little girl run in and out of candle light for a moment. *'Abigail,'* she thought. *'What's she doing here?'* The air grew colder, until she once again saw the frosted breath from her mouth. *'What's happening? Why is it growing so cold?'*

"You must be absolutely devastated. To meet your grandmother only to have her taken from you." Esmeret stared at Lily with cold gray eyes. Ozy bent to pour her a glass of wine and the Smiling Lady waved him away. There was something about her that reminded Lily of the way a preying mantis creeps up on its victim

"And to be the lassssst of your kind, don't forget that," Kadru hissed.

Villon chuckled then, a sound that didn't belong in the dining room the big, creaking house. Something told Lily Nightfall Manor hadn't heard much laughter in all the endless years of its existence.

"Forgive me," he said to Lily. "I haven't been in proper company in a long time and I've forgotten how to behave. It's just that we knew your grandmother and I don't think she would be one

216

for romanticizing the relationships she had with those of us who wished her ill."

"What do you mean?" Lily asked. Winter seemed to have crept into the room. The coldness increased around her again. How could the others pretend that they didn't notice it?

"Your grandmother was the fly in our ointment, façon de parler, and the only thing that has held us here for many years," Villon said. "You can imagine the temptation to escape from your cell, especially when you've been locked inside for eons."

"Francois, let us not speak of such unpleasant things," Esmeret said. Her bloodless lips pursed into a frown.

"Why not? Do you think we're deceiving this child by pretending we want to do anything but rip her throat from her body?" Villon said.

"There are rules that were established, promises made that we can't unbind," she said. Her voice was as quiet as a stream gurgling over a brook in deep woods.

"Rules that were made to ensure we're never free of this cursed place," Villon said. He turned to Lily. "Would you really like to know about your grandmother?"

Lily said nothing, but Villon continued as though she had given him her approval.

"Your grandmother was a tired old gasbag who lost her mind when her husband died, but even then we couldn't get to her. She sniffed out the poisons we put in her food. She dodged the arrow an assassin loosened against her. Our blackest magic couldn't penetrate Nightfall Manor. Deiva rarely left the house and never walked the Gardens after dark, so there was little chance to catch her unaware. The last of the Blackwoods and we still couldn't get her!" The Frenchman pounded his fist on the table and jostled his wine glass, which slopped over the top.

"Thatssssss enough," Kadru hissed. Her rattle grew louder under the table as though she were about to strike.

"More wine," Villon said. He swallowed the last of his glass and set it on the table.

"You don't need more," Esmeret said.

"Don't tell me what I need. I'm not some human you can suck dry like squeezing the juice from a peach," Villon said.

Ozy poured another glass of wine for the Frenchman. When he was finished, Villon held his cup in the air. "All hail the last female Blackwood of Nightfall Gardens." With that he tipped his glass back and drank it dry. Esmeret and Kadru scowled at him in response.

Lily felt fear and anger bubbling inside of her. This arrogant boy from the White Garden was acting as if her grandmother's death should have happened sooner. Now he was mocking her with his salute. She opened her mouth to defend her family and that was when it happened. The intense cold grew so powerful that her teeth began chattering. Next, the candles flickered on the table before being snuffed out and the room was plunged into darkness. A glass shattered, followed by a chair being knocked over. Polly screamed, "Where are you, miss? Where are you?"

Lily's heart pounded. She had passed fear and entered a territory of horror that she hadn't known existed. The house was supposed to protect her, but it had failed, and now she was going to die. What she did next was pure instinct. Lily slid out of the chair, prepared to flee. She hadn't taken more than a handful of blind steps when cold talon-like fingers pressed tight against her arm. A soft voice spoke over her shoulder. "It's been many years since I've tasted Blackwood blood." Esmeret whispered. Icy lips pressed against her throat and ran down her neck. She smelled rank graveyard breath and felt sharp fangs probe her throat. All the strength fled from her. The Smiling Lady pulled her close, her long fingernails stroking Lily's throat, before landing on Deiva's necklace. As soon as her fingers touched the necklace, Esmeret screamed with intense pain. Her lips flew off Lily's neck and her hand loosened its grip. Footsteps pounded out of the room and the front door opened and slammed as the Smiling Lady fled into the gardens. *What did I do?* Lily thought.

"Hold on miss, we're coming for you," Polly said in the darkness. "Not my poor sweet Lily. They'll pay for this, they will," the housemaid said.

"Willll weeeee?" a voice hissed, followed by the

sound of a dry rattle. Kadru was somewhere nearby. Lily held her breath. The sound of the tail swished across the floor and the rattle grew closer.

"Wherrrrre are you?" the snake woman asked. "The last of the Blackwood women and the housssse is too weak to keep ussss out now that we're in."

Lily listened for the sound of the rattle but suddenly it grew quiet and there was no noise. Everything in the room was holding its breath.

At that moment, a candle was lit. Lily saw Ozy with a match, bending low to light another one. The second thing she saw was Polly with her mouth open, about to scream. If Lily hadn't glanced at the wall at that moment she might have died. On the wall behind her, she saw the elongated shadow of woman with a snake's body creeping up on her about to strike. Lily jumped to the side as the shadow struck and Kadru grasped at air where she had been. Lily hit the ground and rolled on her side. She scraped her elbow and ripped her dress as she came back to her feet.

"Long yearsssss. Long yearsssss of torture," Kadru said. "And now it all endsssss." The rattling sound was so loud that Lily could hear nothing else. She backed against the wall as the snake-woman slithered toward her. Her claws were dripping poisonous green pus. The creature loomed over her for the kill.

"It's too early for this yet," Villon said appearing next to Kadru. He was swigging from a bottle of wine. "Let the girl go. We made a promise nothing would happen here." The drunken fool from earlier was gone and in his place was someone who appeared many years older.

"Never! We agreed to thisssss. To kill her! We'll be free once and for all," Kadru said. She slithered closer to Lily pushing Villon out of the way.

"I'm afraid I can't let that happen," Villon said. He moved so quickly that Lily was caught off guard. One moment he was drinking from the bottle of wine and the next his hands were around Kadru's throat. The snake-woman cried out slashing at him and bucking, but his hands clamped tighter until they penetrated the flesh like fingers squeezing wet mud. Kadru screamed one final time as Villon yanked her head from her body and flung it to the flagstones, where it bounced and rolled to the hem of Lily's dress.

Lily opened her mouth to scream but nothing came out. Polly was at her side then, glaring through narrowed white slits at Villon. "What kind of evil have you brought into this house? Never happened before. The house is supposed to protect us." The slug put her arms around Lily's shoulders and Lily felt sticky slime trickle down her arms.

"The dark is growing stronger," Villon said. "Before long, the Gardens will fall and once that happens, the house will be next. Then the world will be plunged into chaos as a new dark age begins."

Lily looked at him. There was no time for shock,

no time to mourn the loss of who she used to be. In the last minutes, everything clarified itself. Paris would have to wait. She couldn't let the creatures she'd seen tonight out into the world.

"Why did you save me?" she asked after she'd caught her breath.

Villon smirked. "What makes you so sure I'm doing that? You will have wished Kadru had gotten hold of you if you aren't able to stop this. The end prophecy said that the Gardens will fall when the last Blackwood female dies. But not all of us that live here want the old days to return. Besides, I could never resist une belle gueule."

He walked towards the door. "Tell no one what I did and go ahead with the burning tonight. Remember, you are a Blackwood and those creatures fear you as much as you do them."

With that, Villon disappeared and left Lily, Polly and Ozy alone. Polly was crying tears of ooze. She wiped her face on her sleeves and slimy tears dripped to the floor. Lily suddenly felt sorry for the housemaid. "What's wrong, Polly?"

"The dark days are coming, miss. Thought I could avoid 'em, I did. But you can't avoid the world around you."

"We'll get through this," Lily said, wondering if it were true.

The bonfire was lit an hour later in view of the three gardens. The pit had been built by the dusk riders during the previous day. A coffin nestled on top of a huge stack of kindling. The box was open and her grandmother's hands were clasped across her chest. The spark of life had left her physical form many hours before. A sprinkle of rain was falling as the first logs took fire and spitted to life. The flames licked hungrily at the wood and soon a blaze was going. Lily watched from her grandmother's old room. She caught one last glimpse of Deiva before her grandmother's body was engulfed in flames. Thousands of eyes watched from the gardens as their old nemesis burned to ash.

"A pity," Polly said, watching with her.

"What is?" Lily asked.

"This world," the slug woman said.

They watched until the embers burned low and then Polly said goodnight. "Must be up early to clean up the mess downstairs," she said. "Get some sleep, miss. Everything looks better after a couple of hours of shut-eye."

Lily waited until she left the room. Once she was sure she was alone, Lily took out Abigail's diary and stared at the strange symbols in front of her. The red moon rose to its height outside of her window. Lily slipped out the Gorgon Claw that Raga had given her. Raga had told her that spilling her blood on the book when the red moon reached its zenith would reveal its secrets. She pressed the claw against her palm and tried not to wince as she sliced it open and her blood dropped on the pages where it was greedily soaked up by the book. When she finished, Lily wrapped a cloth around her hand and took the book to the window. In the moonlight, the symbols changed shape and were now words upon the page. She read for little more than half an hour before tears were falling from her eyes at the sad tale in front of her. *'This can't be true,'* she thought as she closed the book to mull over what she'd learned. If what Abigail had written was true, then even darker times lay ahead for her and Silas.

14
Journey to the Mist

"I don't remember, lad," Jonquil said with a shake of his head. He and Silas were walking the path between the Shadow Garden and the Labyrinth. It was early afternoon and gray, dismal light fell from the sky reflecting their emotions. More than three weeks had passed since Jonquil had drunk the potion made from Fairy Bells. Silas's uncle was growing stronger by the day, but he was still a shadow of his former self. His face was gaunt, and the scar that ran along his cheek gleamed whiter than the rest of him. Jonquil used a staff to support himself and the wolf cloak was pulled tightly about him at all times, as if the cold was invading his bones. His memory was also spotty. Jonquil could recall everything up to the time he and the other riders had gone north into the mist, but then his memories were as patchy as the land they had traveled through.

"It's like when you dream," Jonquil said as they continued their afternoon walk. "When it's happening it feels vivid and real, but when you wake, you can only recall one or two details. I remember riding into Priortage, the largest village of the mist people. I have a memory of being inside an abandoned cottage. I remember signs drawn on trees in blood to warn strangers away." Jonquil shook his head as if it hurt him to recollect what had taken place. "I think we were following Eldritch. Then everything grew dark until I awoke back here."

They came to a clearing between the gardens and found a spot to take a break. "Blast it all. If only I remembered," his uncle said. He laid the staff across his legs as he sat in the grass. "I'm afraid there's nothing to do but go back and talk with the villagers again. If Eldritch is on the loose, then no one is safe."

"You're in no condition to go back there," Silas said. "Perhaps you could send Arfast or Skuld?"

"Nay, lad. I need Skuld and Arfast to keep the camp in check. And if it's true what you said about one of the dusk riders being in league with the wolves, it seems there's truly no one else to trust."

Silas told his uncle about what he'd seen on the night that he'd followed the dusk rider into the woods and saw him talking with the white wolf.

"In some ways that's more troubling than Eldritch being back. For if the wolves are working to bring the three gardens together and some of the riders are helping them, things are much worse than I suspected."

"So when will you go?" Silas asked.

"Soon, lad. Every second I delay the power of the darkness grows stronger."

"Who will you take with you?"

"I'm glad you asked, because there are precious few on whom I can depend. I want you to go with me."

"Me?" Silas said. He was caught off-guard. Ever since he had come here, Jonquil had made sure his nephew was out working with Mr. Hawthorne in the Gardens, reminding him that it would be a long period before he would become a dusk rider.

"I can see the shock on your face, so let me explain. I'm not able to get around as quickly as I once could. I need extra eyes and ears to guide me." Jonquil took his staff and began digging into the earth. "We would be going into treacherous country. This is a decision you'll have to make of your own free will. If I had another choice I wouldn't ask, but we're past the point of pretending that there is time to do things the normal way. So which will it be? If you say nay, then no one will be the wiser."

Silas thought of the peril ahead. The mist was just as dangerous as the gardens. It was full of wolves and other evils that escaped over the centuries. Worst of all, Eldritch loomed somewhere at the end of the mist where it faded into nothingness. Silas thought of the reports coming from the villages; of families found with the life stolen from their bodies, of missing villagers, and of the bloodshed that was happening. It wasn't right for him to stay behind if he could offer something to help. Still, he was afraid and it took him a moment before he said, "I'll go with you. We must stop this."

"That's a good lad. Spoken like a true Blackwood. Your father and I once rode into the mist when we were younger to track down a goblin that escaped from the White Garden. But that's a story for another day."

Jonquil tried to climb to his feet, but his legs buckled and Silas reached down and pulled his uncle up by his arms. *'He needs to rest,'* Silas thought. *'We won't stand a chance if we run into Eldritch.'*

They walked back toward the bunkhouse. "When will we leave?" Silas asked.

"Tomorrow. I wish we could wait longer, but there isn't time," Jonquil said. "You need to tell Mr. Hawthorne you'll be gone, and then go up to the house and see your sister."

"The house!" Silas said excitedly. He hadn't seen his sister since they had first come to Nightfall Manor, months earlier. Even when Deiva died, he hadn't been able to go to Lily because he and Arfast were gathering Fairy Bells and by the time they'd gotten back it was too late. When he asked to see her on the night of his grandmother's funeral, his uncle denied his request. "The house is for her and out here is for you," Jonquil said in his raspy voice. "Soon you'll understand."

Silas almost danced all the way back to the bunkhouse, where he helped Jonquil find a seat next to the fireplace so he could warm himself.

"We leave early, lad. Don't be out too late," his uncle said. Silas promised he wouldn't and ran to Mr. Hawthorne's where he hoped to find the gardener. Instead, when he banged on the door, Cassandra opened it, a gleam of anger in her eyes when she saw who it was. Osbold flew down from the rafters and perched on her shoulder, making cooing sounds.

"What do *you* want?" she glared.

"I'm looking for your father," Silas said.

"Well, it's obvious he's not here," she said. "He's in the hothouse working on his experiments. Why do you need him?"

"I'm leaving tomorrow for the mist lands with Jonquil," Silas said. He told her of Eldritch and the other things happening in the land to the north.

"Never were one much for common sense, were you?" Cassandra said, but her eyes softened and she reached out to touch him on the cheek before she caught herself and brought her hand back to her side. "Take care of yourself," she said. "And don't be as stupid as you normally are."

"Thanks for the compliment," he said angrily. He wondered if he'd ever figure the green girl out. One minute she was ready to cut him to the quick and the next she was all warmth and honey. Neither mood ever lasted long.

Silas went past the barn to Mr. Hawthorne's laboratory. The hothouse was where the gardener came up with the potions for his spell box and studied the strange plants and flowers that grew in the garden. It was something his family had done for hundreds of years. All of the wisdom they collected was written down in a large leather book of yellowed pages. When he entered, he found Mr. Hawthorne bent over a microscope, examining a gold and red leaf that wriggled on a slide in front of him. He looked up when Silas entered; a smile broke across his face and his bushy mustache pulled back to reveal uneven teeth.

"Well hello, lad. To what do I owe the honor? I thought you were spending the day with your uncle," Mr. Hawthorne pushed back from the microscope and stood. "I was just about to take a break anyway. I'm studying mangler vines to find out if there's anyway we can neutralize what makes them so dangerous. I've logged dozens of deadly plants and flowers in the garden. Imagine if they could all be turned to the good."

Silas brushed over what Mr. Hawthorne told him. "Actually, there's something I need to tell you," he said, filling the groundskeeper in on what he could.

"There's a lot happening right now that doesn't make sense," Mr. Hawthorne said when Silas finished. "The Gardens are more restless than ever.

Even the plants within them are growing more quickly and wildly. I've discovered several new species in the last few weeks. I don't envy you, lad. What's happening right now beats everything I've seen. But if you're going to go, at least let me give you a couple of things that might help."

Mr. Hawthorne rummaged through his work bench and came up with a satchel that he started filling. "Warlock grass. No matter how dark or misty, if you light this it can be seen for miles around. Put a drop of this pure grain in your Uncle Jonquil's morning tea and it'll help him regain his strength. This tracker spray is made from skull cap and will cover your scent if something's on your trail."

The groundskeeper put the items in the sack and handed it to Silas. "And remember, if you're lost in the woods, the buldaberry root provides sustenance. Just dig near the roots of Iron Bark trees and you should find it."

"Thanks, Mr. Hawthorne," Silas said. "I'll come back to help as soon as I can."

"I know you will," Mr. Hawthorne said. "Just make sure to protect yourself."

The last light was fading by the time Silas reached Nightfall Manor. As usual, the house seemed to have sprouted whole new wings and a spire jutted from one corner of the house that he was sure hadn't been there the day before. He thought of his sister locked up in this strange house and wondered how she had been doing. He knocked on the front door and it was opened by a tiny woman with a unibrow and a wart on her cheek. She smiled with a lopsided grin, her lank hair falling over one of her eyes. Instantly, Silas felt his mood fall and he was overcome with a powerful depression. The forces that were aligned against him and his sister felt too strong to beat, and even if they did, they would be stuck here for the rest of their lives. And speaking of that, what was life about anyway? The gloom crushed in on him and he would have broken down into tears, except just then Ursula spoke.

"Beautiful day, innit? All ghastly and gray, just the way I like it." The glumpog lead him inside and up a flight of stairs. "The mistress will be glad to see you, she will. She expected you a might earlier though."

"Expected me?" Silas said, trying to keep from bursting into tears.

"Aye. Your uncle Jonquil sent a message a while ago. You won't believe how your sister's changed. Got rid of all that color she had when you first arrived and got a nice graveyard sheen now. Thin as a rail too. You can really see her bones poking out. Nothing more handsome than a skeleton, I say."

They came to the door where his grandmother had been and Ursula turned to leave. "She's in there. She'll be right pleased at how you look as well."

Silas wondered what that meant, but the

hopelessness he felt overwhelmed him and he couldn't say anything. Only when Ursula was gone did his normal mood return. He opened the door, freezing when he saw Lily on the other side of the room. His grandmother's room had been transformed since his last visit. The table with moldy food was gone and everything looked neat and tidy. A huge fire blazed in the fireplace, heating the room and driving out the perpetual chill that clung about Nightfall Gardens. Ursula was wrong about Lily. Yes, she was paler than when they lived with sunlight, but if anything, the trouble they had been through over the last months had made her more beautiful. Her hair was tied in a ponytail with one curl slipped loose and she wore a white shirt and a pair of riding pants that fit tight against her slight frame. In one hand, she held a sword that she jabbed at a dummy that hung from the ceiling by a chain. He had never seen his sister look so determined and was caught off guard by how her time here had changed her as much as it had him.

"Lily!" he said. In the next second, they were rushing to each other and embracing.

"You've gotten taller," she said turning his head side to side. "Haven't had a haircut in a while either."

"We both look different on that account," he said, a feeling of relief washed over him, that his sister was okay.

"That we do," she said, leading him to the chairs

by the window.

"What are you doing?" he asked.

"Practicing. Every morning Skuld comes to train me in self defense," Lily said. "There are many things out there in the dark that would love to get their hands on the last female Blackwood."

Silas wondered what his father and mother would think. The Lily sitting in front of him was completely different from the vain spoiled girl he had grown up with. There was a toughness he hadn't seen before, and a haunted look to her eyes.

They spent several hours talking about all of the things they had seen and experienced.

"More than one time I thought I was dead," Lily said. "But I always managed to get through it. I feel prepared now, more readied to face what's coming."

"What about Abigail's diary? What did you find there?" Silas said. He looked at the fireplace where the logs were starting to burn low. Outside, night pressed against the panes of glass and far in the distance a wolf howled.

"Still too early to say, I've only just started with it and what I've read I'd rather keep to myself until I figure out if it's true or not. I won't be alone, though. I have you and Cassandra to help me. What about Jonquil?"

Silas took a deep breath. "I don't know. Jonquil thinks his memory will come back once we're in the mist."

"I wish you didn't have to go there," she said.

"I wish I didn't have to either, but it's got to be done. Does Polly or anyone know why the house didn't protect you or why Villon saved you?"

"I've sworn Polly and Ozy to secrecy," she said. "The house won't be strong enough to fend off the forces coming from the outside for much longer. That's why I've got to read Abigail's diary and see if she knew where Pandora's Box was hidden. If one of the creatures from the Gardens finds it first, no one will be safe. According to the prophecy, once the last of the old gods is released from the box, the Gardens will fall and the world will be drowned in darkness."

Silas shuddered. "We have to stop that," he said.

"We'll do the best we can," she said. "It seems overwhelming, but I try to remind myself that we're Blackwoods. There's nothing we can't do, dad used to say."

"He did at that," Silas said.

Finally it came time to leave. Silas gave Lily a last hug and headed toward the door. "May the light follow you even in the deepest dark," Lily said, as Silas was about to leave. "You too," he said. "Take care of yourself. I'll visit as soon as I get back."

"You'd better," Lily said. "I'm the lady of the house now and I'm ordering you to come see me as often as you can."

"I will," Silas said giving her a smile.

That night, he tossed and turned on his bunk for many hours before sleep finally came. He woke to

Jonquil prodding him in the side with his staff. "Get up, boy. The day's not getting younger."

Silas ate a quick breakfast and rolled his few belongings into a sack. By the time he made it outside, Jonquil was already saddled on his white horse. He wasn't the only one. Looking angry enough to spit claw nails, Larkspur's massive bulk was planted on top of a horse that looked as if its knees would buckle at its overburdening load. And another dusk rider, Dan Trainer, was sitting on a dappled horse. Trainer had a pockmarked face and ears that hung all the way to his Adam's apple. Silas hardly knew him.

"Glad you decided to join us, boy," Larkspur said. "I'd hate to have to delay our vacation to the beautiful mist lands. Once you've seen 'em, you'll never want to again." He spit into the dirt and glared at Jonquil.

The rest of the dusk riders gathered in front of the bunkhouse to see the four of them off. A black pony was brought out and Silas climbed on top. Skuld and Arfast came over to talk with him. Skuld laid his one arm on the horse and began to stroke its muzzle. "This is my baby here," he said. "She rides like the wind when she needs to and has sure feet even in the mist. Watch your back out there, lad."

Arfast grinned and punched Silas on the shoulder. "This'll be nothing as bad as the White Garden. The worst you'll have to defend yourself against is the village girls. But if you do run into anything, remember to keep your head. If you stay calm, you can always outwit your opponent," he said winking.

Silas didn't have time to respond before Jonquil was calling out to the assembled group.

"There are dark days approaching," he said. "But the dusk riders have faced them before and we will face them again. Always keep your aim true and your heart pure and everything else will follow." With that he kicked his horse into gear and led the four of them off the hill toward the trees. Silas fell in at the back of the group, behind Dan Trainer. He could hear Larkspur complaining bitterly to Jonquil as they rode. "Don't know why I have to come along," he said. "Any of the riders would have been faster than me."

"And not as many of them need to be kept out of trouble," Jonquil said as they followed the trail into the trees.

Silas looked back once before he was swallowed by the mist and saw the peaks and gables of Nightfall Manor rising above the three gardens. It looked like a house full of secrets. At the bunkhouse, the riders were filing back inside or saddling up for the morning ride. Movement on the hill where Mr. Hawthorne lived caught his attention and he was surprised to see Cassandra standing there with one hand shading her eyes as if she were looking straight at him. Osbold flew above her in circles. The green girl raised her hand and waved. He waved back as the tendrils of mist swirled around him and then she was gone from sight. He hoped she'd seen him. Then he gave a silent prayer that his sister would be safe. With that, he turned and followed his uncle and the others into the mist until they disappeared into the white fog.

ACKNOWLEDGMENTS

No book is written in a vacuum and this one couldn't have been finished without my beautiful wife Kim, who nudged me out of bed before dawn, was my first reader and encouraged me when I was filled with doubt. You inspire me with the generosity and love you bring to our family.

To Blaine Palmer for being a faithful reader and best friend and always telling me what he thinks about my writing. There's a little of your magic in this book.

Frank Sentner, thanks for pouring over the manuscript with a fine tooth comb and for raising such an amazing daughter.

Marissa Maier, your early suggestions helped shape the beginning and informed the rest of the novel.

To Tony Roberts for helping to bring my story to life in your illustration.

I had a great proofreader and editor in the indomitable Regan Hoffman. Thanks so much for your hard work and feedback on where you thought the book went right and strayed from the path.

Jason Heid, my old compadre. You read your way through a lot of my writing, never complaining, always supportive. Thanks.

Romeo Alaeff, how many countless hours have we spent talking about art and writing? From Dallas to Berlin, thanks for having my back.

A shout out goes to my brother Grant. Nightfall Gardens is a throwback to the stories I used to tell when we were children. No wonder it was so hard for you to fall asleep.

Finally, I'd like to thank the kids. Lily Rodgers for being my first under 10 reader and badgering me about when the second book was coming out. And Lily Butler, Oggie Johnson, Roman Meek and Abigail Flynn. Children of friends. The future is yours.

ABOUT THE AUTHOR

Allen Houston is a native Oklahoman who has lived in Japan and Indonesia. He has worked as a journalist at the *Dallas Morning News* and *New York Post*. He's currently city editor for *Metro New York*. Allen lives in Brooklyn with his wife, daughter and a menagerie of animals.

CPSIA information can be obtained
at www.ICGtesting.com
Printed in the USA
LVHW111308290722
724664LV00004B/140